Bernard Cohen is the author of five previous novels – *Tourism, The Blindman's Hat, Snowdome, Hardly Beach Weather* and *The Antibiography of Robert F. Menzies* – and the children's book *Paul Needs Specs.*

The Blindman's Hat won *The Australian/*Vogel Literary Award and *The Antibiography of Robert F. Menzies* was the inaugural winner of the Russell Prize for Humour Writing. Bernard is the only writer to appear three times on the *Sydney Morning Herald*'s Best Young Australian Novelists list.

In 2006, Bernard founded The Writing Workshop. Since then, he has taught creative writing to over 75,000 young people. His website is at www.bernardcohen.com.au, or see www.writingworkshop.com.au for more information on Bernard's teaching. Instagram: @bernardcohen1

He lives in Sydney.

ALSO BY BERNARD COHEN

Tourism
The Blindman's Hat
Snowdome
Hardly Beach Weather
Paul Needs Specs (children's picture book)
The Antibiography of Robert F. Menzies

PRAISE FOR BERNARD COHEN

'Cohen makes the urban landscape as beautiful as a Jeffrey Smart painting ... but there is an unnerving sense of menace in the glistening horizontals and verticals.' *The Age*

'Eclectic, paranoid and barbed ... brilliantly original.' *Mail on Sunday* (UK)

'Cohen has a capacity for serious analysis of contemporary urban culture; he is equally merciless as social commentator or psychological profiler and his deadpan humour is always on target.' *Newcastle Herald*

'Terrific writing: funny, cutting and wonderfully accurate.' *Newtown Review of Books*

'Cohen takes up the interconnected preoccupations of modern life and subjects them to intense and witty scrutiny.' *Adelaide Advertiser*

'Brilliant and importantly distinctive writing.' Brenda Walker

WHEN I SAW
THE ANIMAL

BERNARD COHEN

UQP

First published 2018 by University of Queensland Press
PO Box 6042, St Lucia, Queensland 4067 Australia

uqp.com.au
uqp@uqp.uq.edu.au

Cover design by Josh Durham, Design by Committee
Cover photograph by Josh Durham/Bigstock
Author photograph by Mira Lemberg @mirabellaphotog
Typeset in Bembo Std 11/15pt by Post Pre-press Group, Brisbane
Printed in Australia by McPherson's Printing Group, Melbourne

 **Queensland** This project is supported by the Queensland
Government Government through Arts Queensland.

  The University of Queensland Press is
assisted by the Australian Government
through the Australia Council, its arts
funding and advisory body.

ISBN 978 0 7022 6021 6 (pbk)
ISBN 978 0 7022 6157 2 (pdf)
ISBN 978 0 7022 6158 9 (epub)
ISBN 978 0 7022 6159 6 (kindle)

 A catalogue record for this
book is available from the
National Library of Australia

For Tamara and Tali

Contents

PART I

PART I

Gilberto

Everything around that dining table was as normal as clouds contorting in the sky. Dad was pacing up and down, looking at his phone, putting it in and taking it out of his trouser pocket, looking at it again like some poorly directed extra. Mum sat at the far end of the table as the steam dissipated from her serve of mashed potato. She was poking at the food with her fork, and sort of eating it in that semi-polite way of beginning while not wanting to begin before we had all sat down. Belinda was testing to see if she could cut the meat while holding the fork in her right hand and knife in her left, and the proof she couldn't was the small scattering of potato on the table beside her drinking glass.

I wasn't there yet but would be soon, and when I arrived oh boy would their demeanours shift. Just wait.

'Sorry about this being late,' I said, on my first step past the dining-room door. 'I didn't mean it at all. And also the making-you-wait thing. Not what I wanted to happen, but there is a reason.'

'Bloody, bloody,' said Belinda. 'Here we go again.'

'Is that language completely necessary?' rehearsed Dad.

'Necessity component 94.3 per cent,' said Belinda. 'So no. Not completely.'

'Sit down, Blake,' said Mum. 'Let's at least eat while we endure your poor excuse.'

Dad and I took our places, and Dad immediately began to eat his potato with a teaspoon.

'Anyway,' I said, 'as I was walking home from school, I saw a man walking two magnificent dogs of great stature, the breed of which I happened to recognise, due to my patronage last weekend of the *Dogs of the World* TV special, as Kazakhstani wolfhounds.'

'Shaggy dog story,' said Belinda, categorically.

'*Short*-haired Kazakhstani wolfhounds,' I corrected. 'I engaged this man in conversation by asking rhetorically, "Are those Kazakhstani wolfhounds?" and he seemed very pleased by this recognition. No knowledge is bad knowledge, right Dad?'

'Hrrrmpphh,' assented Dad, through his ongoing mouthful.

'The man told me his sad story, that he and his brother had each taken one puppy, but that his brother had died of some rare virus, and so he walked the two dogs with a heavy heart. He actually used the phrase "heavy heart". I asked if the dogs were friendly, and began to scratch one of them behind its ears. This particular dog took an immediate liking to me.'

'Dr Do-nothing.' Belinda couldn't not say things, in case that wasn't obvious enough.

'Thanks. So what did you do today?'

'Plenty,' she lied.

'So the man said, "He seems so fond of you. His name is Gilberto. I renamed him after my late brother." I told him how lovely that was, and the man said to me, "You know, two dogs is really too much for me, and it's so sad every day. Would you like Gilberto? But no, you probably already have a dog."'

My family were perhaps more attentive at this moment than at any time in history. I swept my hand grandly around its full arc.

'You didn't,' said Mum.

'I did. I said to him, "That's so beautiful."'

'No,' said Belinda.

'And so … we've got a dog. Who wants to help me bathe him after dinner?'

'You have to give it back,' said Mum. 'We're not dog people.'

'Just have a look at him, Mum,' I pleaded. 'I guarantee you'll fall in love.'

'I've never fallen in love before,' said Mum, pointedly not looking at Dad, 'so I think that's unlikely. You'll have to take it back.'

'I actually can't,' I said. 'I have no idea where the guy lives or his name or anything. But just have a look at him.'

'Don't worry, Mum. He's only having us on,' said Belinda.

'I'll help you bathe him,' said Dad, unexpectedly.

At that moment Gilberto let out a massive yowl from where I'd tied him up out the front. I don't recall ever having seen Dad look so happy. Belinda just stared at me like she couldn't believe I'd told the truth. I always tell the truth, so what was with that?

'We had a Great Dane when I was a teenager,' Dad said. 'The old type, before all the wolf was bred out of them.'

'No,' said Mum.

'It would take over the entire house,' said Belinda. 'Are you going to keep it in your room?'

'I don't mind,' I said. 'He'll probably decide himself where he goes. You can walk him sometimes if you want. If he likes you, that is.'

'He's going to the pound,' said Mum. 'You can put up notices around the area so the owner can find him again.'

'I'm the owner,' I said. 'And I don't need to find him.'

'Look,' Dad said in the conciliatory voice he uses when he knows he's about to say completely the wrong thing, 'why don't we give the dog a try for a couple of weeks? If it doesn't work for all of us, we can figure out what to do with him after that.'

'That seems reasonable,' I said quickly. They'd never be able to get rid of him once they'd met him.

'No,' said Mum again. 'There will be no dog.'

'I'm with Mum,' said Belinda. 'Dogs smell houses out. It will be revolting and after a few weeks we won't even notice how squalid everything has become. We'll lose all our friends and all their replacements will be weirdos we meet in the park who've also lost all their friends because of the dog-stink thing.'

'So negative,' I said.

Gilberto yowled again, almost impossibly loudly, though the increased volume was immediately explained when he came running into the dining room, trailing his chewed-through rope. Dad leapt to his feet, Mum instinctively covered her food with a piece of paper towel, and Belinda did that folding-up thing that people do to reduce surface area available for licking or sniffing at. As always, this motion had the opposite effect to that intended, and Gilberto went straight up to Belinda, his brontosauric tail wagging with potential destruction.

'Help!' said Belinda.

'Gilberto, here boy! Come here!' I shouted.

Dad came around the table, and we wrestled the dog away from Belinda, but not before a chair or two had been smashed to the ground by his mighty tail translating potential into kinetic energy.

'See. I told you he was lovely,' I said.

Mum returned to her monosyllabic 'No.'

'You know what,' said Dad. 'Yes.'

Mum spun around and stared at him. Her face, which I guess had contained the practised negativity of a high-school debater, became virtually expressionless, the thinnest example of a smile lifting the corner of her mouth by a degree or two.

'You're saying "Yes",' she said, a question without inflection.

'I think I am. No. I *am*,' said Dad, remembering to meet her eyes.

Gilberto had stopped his brutal running around and with a series of limb-folds lay down on a tiled section of the dining room in front of what had been a fireplace.

'Fine,' said Mum. 'You know what this means?'

'Spell it out,' said Dad.

'Crapping bloody crap,' said Belinda, a phrase that doesn't bear thinking about. 'Blake, please.'

I'd left the table and was sitting beside Gilberto, rubbing the hard crest of his skull between the ears.

'I'll write it down,' said Mum, 'in the letter.'

'I'll be sure to write back, in time,' said Dad.

'Blake,' repeated Belinda.

'It's just about the dog for me,' I said lamely, continuing to stroke Gilberto. 'I can't help the rest.'

'Okay,' said Belinda, 'but we all know that's not true. You could have foreseen this. You probably did.'

'Unfair,' I said, because who could possibly foresee which action would have what result in human relations?

Mum and Dad had separately left the room through different doors, and Belinda also stood to leave.

'See you round, Blake,' said my sister.

'Bye,' I said. The whole thing was too bizarre. All this resulting from a dog? It made no sense. I sat there with Gilberto and waited for it all to blow over, for my parents to re-enter with a jointly delivered Yes or the more likely No, for Belinda to retell the story to her friends within my hearing, including me as the fool. I waited for the wonderful Gilberto to be taken from me and for everyone to deliver to me endless lessons about my endless foolishness.

'Anyway, Gilberto,' I said out loud. 'If it was up to me, you and I would keep the house.'

If I had ever imagined that a wish I made would be fulfilled, it would not have been that, just one month later, Gilberto and I *had* kept the house. Instead, it might have been some wishy-washy wish about us all being happy, about which

Belinda would have made uncountable sarcastic remarks. But it was my first-voiced desire which came to pass.

Mum moved out the day I brought Gilberto home, saying, 'It's not you. It's your father.'

Belinda had gone with her, adding only that she would stay with Mum to make sure she was all right.

Or, more exactly, 'Whatever Mum says, or Dad, or the Pied bloody Piper, this is all your fault, Blake. Our parents would have lasted forever but for you and Gilberto, your stupid little pony.'

In fact, Dad lasted no time at all without Mum. He missed her immensely, and for all his sense that he was a dog person who had been deprived of dogs for two decades, he completely folded – or as completely as he could. I guess Belinda was right and my dog-lovingness had been a catalyst for their separation. I had somehow convinced Dad that it was too late for Gilberto to be sent anywhere: there was nowhere to send him back to, and the only alternative was to send him to a likely death. I asked Dad to imagine poor, hyper-friendly Gilberto being locked in too small a cage at the pound and eventually put down. My father would have done almost anything to make it up with Mum, anything but cause Gilberto harm, but she refused to take Dad back. Within three days of Gilberto's arrival, presumably as some kind of hopeful penance, Dad had gone to live in a dog-free apartment just around the corner from Mum.

This was, I told him, a very bad idea. True penance has no other motives, and I tried to explain to Dad that hopeful penance was bound to be hopeless.

Meantime, I did my best to walk and feed and wash Gilberto, and I tried to pick up and dispose of all the dog poo. Belinda even shifted her nickname for me from Dr Do-nothing to Dr Doodoo – admittedly not much of an improvement, but at least an acknowledgement of my effortfulness. I demonstrated to Mum, Dad and Belinda how close Gilberto and I were, and Gilberto definitely became my dog. I had found a chain he couldn't chew through, and he no longer came into the house without my invitation – though this was frequently proffered and accepted.

Mum and Dad came to visit me most days. Dad brought food and waited for me to come to my senses, which I didn't. Mum brought food and an attitude of understanding and forbearance, but wouldn't enter the house if Gilberto was inside. Belinda brought questions such as, 'Why are you such an idiot, Blake?' and 'You do know that you've destroyed my life and the lives of all those around you?'

Belinda had been right about the house becoming a dog house, and it probably did stink. But none of my friends minded, so I kept them all. I also met many more people fascinated by this massive canine towing a teenager around the neighbourhood every morning and afternoon.

One evening there was a thumping on the door and, as my family would not have bothered to knock and my friends would have tapped in odd or distinctive ways, I assumed it was neither. I opened the door: when you have a dog the size of mine, you forget caution. An older man I had never seen before stood there. He looked a bit knocked about, as though he'd had bruises but didn't any longer.

'Gilberto,' the man said.

'My dog,' I said. 'Is something wrong?'

Gilberto was clattering his chain in an extremely lively way, even for him. The man stuck out his hand.

'Blake,' I said, shaking it.

He nodded, but didn't say his own name. Gilberto had started on the yowling again.

'Just hang on a second,' I said. 'I need to check on my dog.'

'Your dog,' he echoed.

'Gilberto,' I said, turning and running to the backyard.

Gilberto was tugging the chain towards the house with all his might.

'What's up, boy?' I said, unhooking him and completely missing as I went to grab his collar. Gilberto ran for the house. I chased him, calling 'Stop! Stop!' although this had no effect at all. He ran straight for the man who, instead of flinching, dropped to one knee right there on my front step. The dog almost sent him flying, but the man reached out and hugged him like a long-lost relative.

'Gilberto?' I said.

'Yes,' said the man. 'Thank you. I have returned.'

I almost lost the power of speech: 'You? Dead? Not?'

'Not,' said Gilberto the man. 'But I will kill my brother. Though not literally.'

'Why?'

'My brother is a liar, a thief, a swindler,' said Gilberto. 'It's a pity I love him.'

'What?' I asked, still stuck on one word at a time.

'Families are complicated.'

I couldn't disagree with him.

I'd like to report that over the next week, my family moved back in, repaired the furniture, painted the walls, sanded the floor and filled in the holes in the backyard, and all went back to the way it had been. Instead, we instituted a set of trials and tests, with regular reviews and conferences, all scheduled for different evenings in the dining room.

As Belinda told me, 'You just had to do that, didn't you?'

When I Saw the Animal

The first time I saw the animal, I'll admit I was tired. It was late at night and I had been drinking at moderate pace for several hours. The animal could have been anything, the way it flashed across the room, and I was too slow to get a good look at it, as though my eyes had been insulated away from my mud-sozzled brain. Let's hope that wasn't a rat, I thought to myself. Why anyone should have hoped for it not being this over anything else, I couldn't say, and nor, considering I was alone at the time of that first sighting, who the implicit 'us' was. As I said, I was tired, and sometimes sense doesn't have to be made.

Nothing happened for a few days. Perhaps it had been an isolated incident, an anomaly. Perhaps it hadn't been there at all, a trick of the eye or mind, wishful thinking, paranoia, hallucination. After a few days, a false memory.

But no. Some nights later, I half-saw the animal again (or perhaps a different one). It's true that I had once again consumed several drinks that evening, but not so many as to mistrust the evidence of my own perceptions. One sighting could have amounted to a freak happening. Twice constituted the early signs of a pattern.

The next day I purchased a rat-trap. Setting traps was not an activity with which I had previously been familiar, so I was meticulous in following the instructions on the rat-trap's packaging. Despite widespread depictions, it seems that cheese is not the most effective enticement for rodents of any size. I set the trap with a small piece of meat. Rats are, as further attested to by the packaging, neophobes, and I prepared myself to wait several days for this particular one to work up the courage to get itself killed. In addition to occupying a chair from which I had a reasonable view of the trap, I checked the trap many times a day. I did not touch or move it which, so I had read, would likely have reduced the trap's effectiveness.

Initially I'd been satisfied with the whole of my enterprise, but the trap was not successful. It trapped nothing, not even the slug which had worn away at the food scrap one evening and trailed off across the carpet, still in one piece. I was pleased not to trap the slug, which would have been unpleasant, though it was disappointing not to have trapped the rat, if that's what it had been. Perhaps or probably, I concluded, given that no rat had been captured, the animal had not been a rat. The absence of a rat would explain the failure of the rat-trap. And if the animal had not been a rat, so I reasoned, it was best not to have trapped it.

Life slowly returned to its previous pre-mammalian form. Nothing disturbed my living room for the next seven well-observed nights. The rat-trap had either been a false step or a complete success as a deterrent. Either way, I wrapped the trap in an old piece of plastic, and tucked it at the back of the cupboard under the kitchen sink. With a glass in hand, I returned to the lounge chair. All was quiet. I could have imagined it, the whole thing, the animal, its paths, its peripherality. If I stopped imagining things, it would be for the better. People like me aren't supposed to imagine things. Imagining things is a bad sign, and nobody likes bad signs.

And yet, one evening later, I couldn't not see what I thought I saw. Surely not! Were there two of the creatures running across the room double-helix style, and was there me, sober as anything? And two nights beyond that, after a single quiet night, not one or two but *three* further little mammalian entities? The whisky level only moderately diminished. One, two, three creatures, and not a single clear sighting. I might have reset the trap, but I wanted first to identify the little mammals. Knowledge before outcome. I substituted a notepad and pen for the trap and meat.

Time passed. Hours, days, the less formal measure of bottles. No resolution. The notepad accumulated tally marks but no details. A tally mark represented a blur, a smear in time. There was nothing clear enough to be detailed. If anything, deterioration: the animal or animals became more common and perhaps a little larger, but also fuzzier, less distinct.

The fact of not getting a good look at them was hard to reconcile with the concrete nature of the world. Why were they always running across the edge of my vision and never through its middle? Why were they always just a bit too fast to see clearly but not too fast not to see at all? Were they watching me, waiting for me not to watch them? If so, what was their purpose, or what was the purpose to which they had been put? Had setting the trap set them off me? Could I redeem myself through leaving food unconnected to trapping? Could I calm them through pure demeanour? These were all very good questions, as I assured myself.

I devised little experiments: I would stare at a certain point for fifteen minutes, in order to test whether the paths of the animals were somehow controlled by the direction of my gaze. I placed elaborate roadblocks designed to funnel the animals towards my field of view. Why did they not appear at those times I had prepared myself, or at least when I had told myself I was ready for their appearance? Why did they only run in or through places or follow routes which had not been readied for them?

The animals were highly intelligent, so I concluded, and they must have waited for me to blink or shift my head before running across. Nothing I did hindered them in any way; no diversion seemed to divert them in the least. If I set up a camera and left the room, there was never anything to be seen. They were clever, these animals, and a little larger each day.

The larger they became, I reasoned, the more difficult it would be for them to maintain their hiding places. I searched the house for holes, burrows, hollows, anything that could have provided shelter. There were no signs of habitation.

Troubling as the complete failure of my investigation to that time had been, much more disturbing was what followed. The animals, if that's what they were, slowed markedly. Their movements loosened and became more languorous. In slowing they acquired a – it was the phrase that came to me – divine grace as they followed these unmarked paths along which they could not be properly seen. And yet with their reduced speed, the creatures became no more visible and observable than they had been. I pursued my attempted surveillance with even more rigour and vigour, but with no success or even promise.

The animals were so large now they loomed from the edges of the room and cast shadows over everything I owned. They flowed from corner to corner alone or in pairs or trios, and always I felt as though I could with the right movement possess them and always I chose wrongly.

My calls to them were more desperate now, a pleading, the repetition of the word 'please', a whimpering which came from within me as though detached from my will. They must have been heartless: their lack of response, their continued pauseless drifting hither and thither, as though they had no will but were nasty earthbound clouds of flesh subject to the whim of a force unseen. I tried to hate them but I couldn't; I only wanted them. Please.

The more they slowed, the more they grew. It was a vindictive non-Darwinian evolution. The room had the impression of being loomed over. The animals perhaps lost some of the grace they had earlier gained. My space diminished and I was pressed into its centre, the centre from which I ought to have been all-seeing. I had given up on my tallying by this point, as there always seemed to be at least one of the animals present, resistant as ever to observation. Despite the animals' size and probably mammalian presence, the room itself became colder. I wore all the clothes I owned, rugged around me, slightly constrictive – but what choice did I have? If these animals were warm-blooded as they seemed, their warmth must have been taken from the air, all currents flowing towards them, sucking the heat from anything available, anything including me.

Violence is not really part of my nature, but I admit I tried violent responses to the continuing attacks by the animal or animals on my comfort and enjoyment of the property. I swung chairs. Eyes closed, I struck out with a fork, almost overbalancing due to the failure to make contact. With my eyes open I could see nothing.

They taunted me with their slow growth. Over time it seemed that the animals were growing together, coalescing, that there were no longer three or even two creatures just beyond my grasp, but a single vast entity. Was this possible? Vastness beyond measure or extent and invisibility brought together in the one entity?

It enveloped me. I desired nothing more than to leave this place, to abandon my home to the great heat-sapping beast and to go anywhere else, to find somewhere beyond its reach. This was the great contradiction: it reached me everywhere and yet I couldn't come close to it.

Did I sleep? Did I wake? Did I move or was I held still? Did I love it as it loved me? Did it feel contempt for me as I resented it? Did it feel? Did I feel?

The numbness started in the pit of my stomach. It spread not by moving to contiguous parts but by establishing little colonies of absence in my knees and shoulders and elbows. It found a dwelling place at the back of my jaw.

There was nothing more to drink. I knew none of this could have been my own doing. It was all caused by this creature which had somehow discovered a path through me, through my body and my being. The numbness at times supplanted the cold and at times amplified it. If only I knew how to summon help. I felt as though I knew nothing anymore. In a prior existence I had had access to knowledge and to methods. Surely this was a true statement.

But I could no longer be certain. The feeling or, rather, the lack of feeling stretched up the back of my head, these formerly tight little colonies now sending out tendrils or (ivy-like) aerial rootlets along my main internal carriageways.

I could feel myself about to fall asleep, but I never did.

War Against the Ungulates[*]

1

Everywhere humans continue to grow unevenly. This lack of consistency has come to be considered 'texture'. They attain different heights, widths, densities and varied pigments. Some display prowess on the sporting field, some demonstrate admirable levels of intellect and many show profound aptitude in the unguided formation of sexual relationships. One can rarely predict with accuracy their rates of progress in any of the measurable paradigms.

The humans pursue diverse activities, forming small but workable trading communities. As the centuries have passed, so have these communities evolved increasingly specialised commercial practices. One can thus trace the development of acts seemingly as simple as the burning and consumption of flesh.

2

Some of the humans are unwell but (unlike the ungulates) will soon recover. Some suffer and (also) hold dissonant

---

[*] I wrote this piece in response to the 2001 UK foot-and-mouth outbreak and to media and UK government responses to it.

attitudes. Some will soon die, and it is our duty to minimise pain.

The sheep are scattered in the field, and the cattle in clumps near the fence. Insect life continues in abundance. Great machines are the pinnacle of human achievement, both for their scale and for their central role in producing lattices and other terrains of convenience.

These days we require a rationale for each failure to govern that which is governable, and each rationale spawns self-perpetuating terms. The cameraman holds (is duty-bound to hold) empirical attitudes, and is not interested in justification.

3

'The Information Age sure is producing a lot of information.'

I love text, how it lies all over the country, how its tonality infects every local and national newspaper equally, how no diagram survives without its gnomic insistences, how it gulps and gulps and swallows formerly productive soil formations and suddenly they are replaced with vistas. What I love least about text is seepage. What I most love about text is particularity. The journalist might have expressed the practice in this way.

4

The war against the ungulates begins with declarations. There is much public discussion of strategy. Should they be stalked or confronted, herded or separated? Should they be burned or buried? Can we eat them?

Arguers are ranged against distinctive landscapes; the

cameraman frames the more seriously and directly affected among them squinting into direct sun. This is not company policy, but neither does policy preclude his approach. Mode of framing is the means by which one identifies a professionally developed photographic aesthetic in digital media.

Experts are lit from the side, their faces a balance of light and shadow, reason and sorcery, illumination and the promise of knowledge's dark depths.

5

The content of fields and paths and disease vectors is harmless to all but abnormally susceptible humans, side-lit experts explain. There is no reason to alter behavioural patterns.

6

The roads crisscrossing the countryside have no history. Instead, they are distinguished by unique technical specifications, sensitively calculated in relation to geological and topographical demands.

The cameraman disseminates this information compassionately: his disclosure may shock those following heritage trails. (Almost certainly it will be faux-shock, as the contemporary citizen cannot be troubled by information other than vicariously on behalf of hypersensitive others.)

At least these drivable myth-lines are open, unlike footpaths sealed shut to protect the soles of human feet from the harmless viral seepage. Camera trucks rumble slowly to each new event, drivers heeding speed restrictions and occasional diversions.

7

Meanwhile, there are problems with unmanned video apparatus. In the cities, surveillance fails to distinguish between the noteworthy and patterns of ordinariness. The problem lies in audience-delivery failure. The cameraman grieves that security-conscious citizens record so many useless hours of unobserved tape. He pities the soft focus and poor framing, and it tears his heart that so much action remains uncentred. Everyone regrets the lack of audience for all these many, many performers, each doing his or her duty (in passing beneath security apparatus), each performer inconsolable.

8

Inside television, there is a city without boundaries in which humans and vehicles move as if at random behind carefully casual reporters. The cameraman is always conscious of governability.

9

Sheep so rarely stray into camera-shot that one usually forgets the countryside exists. This is the accusation from non-urban areas and from those the cameraman thinks of as TV-naive. He is relieved that organisational perceptions are that coverage of the rural is proportionate, and there are sanctioned and dissuasive complaints procedures in place to manage the trickle of dissent.

The cattle are out standing in the field. The farmer's in the dell.

10

The war against the ungulates necessitates rhetoric other than the usual rehearsal of democratic principle given above.

They were 'produced' and are faulty. They have violently lost value, to the extent that they must be propped up. Unfortunately for them, their textual transformation is irreversible. One can mourn the cattle without farmers. Sheep herded, but no one titled 'shepherd'. Highways all over the nation. Camera trucks moving through the countryside. These fires have become a commonplace of the countryside. *I have made it so*, reflects the cameraman.

11

When someone publicly enunciates the term 'unfortunate', violence will be justified. Cameras display glowing red lights, but then the press conference ends, the lights blink off and cameramen straighten to ease backache. There is insufficient disagreement among the humans, and camera trucks disperse in search of authenticity.

12

One refers to the war *against* the ungulates because it is impossible to have war *with* them. They will not acknowledge the situation in which we all find ourselves. Humans at war against the ungulates are at war unilaterally. Marginal humans unilaterally declare themselves at peace. But there is no conventional or radical peace with the unacknowledging ungulates. Instead, is there peace *against* the ungulates?

13

Mobility necessitates war: this is as it has always, always been throughout history. The process is:

1. Humans move;
2. There is war;
3. Then: disease.

Oftentimes, an observer may note deliberate attempts to merge 3 into 2. Humans toss their enemies' contagious bodies over ramparts, smuggle smallpox scars in blankets, infect explosive devices with all manner of transmissible organisms.

14

The cameraman has noticed that in crisis no one acknowledges history, only distinguishes present circumstances. Sadly, the past cannot be reconciled.

15

The roads along which we travel have appeared as if impetuously. They do not follow the routes of ancients who could cope with angles and curves and travelled little except to conquer, and were sick and whose teeth fell out through lack of nutrition, and who practised rituals which may be regained through patient meditation and openness. The ungulates used to be governable but are no longer.

16

The cameraman thinks of his youth, with its scattered memories of normal ruminants wearing grooves along hillsides. The ungulates do not appeal for peace. They do not speak out against the war and (thus) through their silence condone it. They do not seek out humans who share their views. They are confined to certain pastures and they move here and there along roads which have appeared for precisely the purpose of bovid movement.

17

The country is capable of growing some of the best grass in the world, and yet ...

18

Members of the government warn us to drive carefully. An opposition spokesperson applauds the government for its measures to counter viral communication, with the rider that the opposition (had it controlled parliament) would have achieved precisely the same results even sooner.

In times of war, one cannot hope for greater vigour than this barest level of debate. An opposition politician proclaims: 'No one wants unnecessary sacrifice.'

19

The terrain extrudes the most nourishing grass in the world. Its herbivores need eat nothing else. The virus reproduces most rapidly in pigs and is most easily taken up by cattle. Cattle are brought in from the fields and fed something else. Pigs eat slop, are rarely permitted to roam the fells.

20

These pyres disturb the cameraman and they disturb optimum landlines. A fellow professional counsels that low angles easily compensate, that news editors appreciate silhouetting, and that with careful framing, one need not challenge the Golden Ratio. The cameraman does not confess the shapes he perceives in the spaces between corpses. There are multifarious vases and other vessels, sometimes buildings reminiscent of Frank Lloyd Wright's, sometimes primitive representations of human faces. As the flames settle, heat concentrates at the base of the pyres. He hears helicopters. The corpses collapse. The pyre makes a strong diagonal against the sky and the perpendicularity of a background stately home. It is machines that effect the burning and humans stand aghast, complexions of flickering pallor.

21
He is susceptible not so much to the disease as to its images.

22
The locals are hardy, unlike their fearful former visitors (now departed). It is dangerous and unpatriotic to touch the ground. We have been warned that the ungulate pelts are highly infectious. We debate the merits of cooked and raw bones. There are too many available conclusions. The cameraman unfortunately and uncontrollably conflates several crises. The effect is to exaggerate his resilience.

23
Please excuse the assimilative and associative nature of the cameraman's thought.

24

Dark-feathered statisticians fill the treetops or circle impatiently for outcomes in the war against the ungulates.

There are new cases every day. A special 'screen within a screen' on the television tallies the spread of illness. Despite this broadcast of relentless counting, the cameraman is unclear on the precise meaning of 'case'. It seems not to refer to individuals, nor to unanimous or even general ungulate contamination in a location. His friend the journalist informs him 'case' refers to 'observed viral presence' and thus is measured by emplacement of film crews. But then the journalist giggles at the formality of his own expression, which seems inappropriate behaviour in the circumstances.

25

In official statements no one admits unmeasured probability, but without it there can be no such thing as hope. The ungulates cannot hope. One does not discuss hope with veterinarians. Absolute regulation of the ungulates is an already-given necessity, a *sine qua non* of the science.

26

Veterinary epidemiologists have come into their own. The government is pleased with its success in tracking. The cameraman is surprised that the term 'outbreak' has not been preferred over 'case', with the former's connotations of rebellion and call to arms. His surprise persists despite the latter's apparent tendency to minimise infection.

27

When viewing pigs, it is not possible to judge whether facial features are liquefying or simply that the animals are slavering uncontrollably. In broadcasts over the relevant epidemiological period, the map slowly shades inflammation-red.

28

The cameraman jokes to selected friends among the film crews that once the island is fully coloured the red of disease, humans shall regain their licence to move freely. All movement is currently (a) treacherous and (b) equivocally and simultaneously permissible and forbidden. It is patriotic to deny contradiction.

29

The prime minister goes to America to smile. He returns and now appears concerned. He allows himself some happiness. The leader of the opposition tries not to smile. He attempts not to nag. He labours towards positivity, but then flags. He attempts not to undertake a number of other attitudes. He disappoints the cameramen and is insufficiently conflictual.

30

War historians steer away from this discussion. They too understand mobility but they know how to set parameters. (This is a quality the cameraman lacks, the ability to set his own limits. He lacks realism, existing solely in the naturalistic. He has observed war historians through his fixed lens and they have eyed him coldly.)

31

The cattle are queuing. The sheep know not for whom they fall. Drawing on several mediated sources, the cameraman deduces that each case is metonymic of one thousand, seven hundred and seventy-nine beasts, supine.

32

Many humans openly support chemical intervention over the war against the ungulates. (Needles are also favoured for use among the humans, with few opposed.) This, they argue, would obviate the warrior imperative, but their approach is counterintuitive. Humans split into teams, barrackers shouting each other down in good-natured democratic interaction. Journalists applaud civility and regular contributions to the half-hour bulletins.

33

Rational humans cheer for death, believing that risk should be eliminated by conclusive means. Rationalists are also concerned about inconclusiveness, always a risk in peacetime. Our leaders wish to move forward and seek our consent. As the leaders weaken, one may observe rationalists on street corners pursing lips and frowning. They have made their case and can do no more. Consensus remains for progress. Only outsiders are against consensus.

34

The nation continues to grow rich and nutritious grasses. It grows grass. It grows poor and uneven. Grazing animals truck across paved commons. High streets everywhere are the same. Some farmers name their herds, fence, guard; others receive conversations. The cameramen repair to regions where disease can be relied upon.

35

'I am afraid,' the journalist reports, with flat remorselessness, 'the cattle are dead.'

36

The number of new cases is falling; registered persons fell existing cases. Because of the urgency, past and future slaughtered are not shielded from one another. It is not a pleasant disease. (Not like ____? But there are no counter-examples.) The surfaces of their tongues dissolve. The virus destabilises cell governance for its own ends. Pigs sneeze uncontrollably. News editors choose to include cattle mucus. This is all part of the war effort, the cameraman reminds himself.

37

The national grass grows, undisturbed. Virulent organisms are arrayed within the soil. Above ground, cattle await. The sheep are collapsed against their pasture. One cannot estimate the travel time of camera trucks without evidence of their points of origin. Some roads are closed, and this makes accurate reporting more difficult still.

38

The prime minister smiles momentarily. There is no recrimination, only personal sorrow.

Thinking back on the war against the ungulates, the cameraman conjures, first, a logic of bodies and, second, a logic of broadcast rituals. First, the ground will be overlaid with flesh. Second, there will be no conflict, in which case audience size will diminish, and this must be countered.

We are barbarous in outlook and results. There are no longer farmers and nor are there writers. Camera trucks range along the highways in search of tendrils of malaise. We are all contributors to large-scale industries which must be understood in an international context. It is easy, reflects the cameraman, to rubbish national priorities.

Hoverdog

The River Fillmore was not in good shape. It stank bad.
More mud than water, not even real mud. Dead fish swam
by. (Kind of.)

'I wish I didn't see that,' Small Lincoln said. 'Gross.'

'Yep,' I said. I poled my kayak towards them.

'Yep.' Big Lincoln reeled in. (Zilch, of course.)

'Whoa,' said the same boy. 'Look at.'

'How the,' said Small Lincoln, same vessel.

'What?' I said.

'Up there.' Small Lincoln jabbed a paddle. Dogwards.
Wilson (terrier) was somehow in a tree.

'Whoa,' I said. 'What the.'

'How the flack,' said Big, making mad signs.

Some kid laughed – but out of sight.

'Show y'self.'

No one appeared.

'Come out, kid,' I said.

The laughter stopped. Silence.

'I'll count to six,' growled Big.

Nothing.

'Six?' queried Small.

'Whatever.'

It was way hot to paddle. Hat brims dripped. The Lincolns' boat drifted. It drifted under that dog.

Wilson yelped. The kid laughed. Everything was slo-mo as. The dog. It fell.

Small Lincoln ducked. Big flinched hard. Wrong moves. Over they went. The River Fillmore. Boys in, dog in. Hats off. Dog snatched hat. Big Lincoln grabbed the dog.

'I can't swim, you bastard.' Shouting, now spluttering. Would the dog keep him up? But Wilson wanted the hat. It was towing him.

'I. (Gulp.) Can't. (Gulp.) Swim.'

They reached shore. Big Lincoln hanging on to the dog. Small Lincoln all arms. Big Lincoln grabbed Wilson. Bearhug. The dog yelped.

'I love you, Wilson,' he said. He kissed it on the eye.

'Gross,' said Small Lincoln. 'I wish I didn't see that.'

'He saved me.' Big started to cry. 'He did.'

I paddled up to them. Two strokes and up. 'Truman Kayak.' Fibreglass on gravel: *schhhht*.

A twig cracked.

'Kid! There!' shouted Small. 'There he goes. Get him!'

The kid flew for it.

Short Twos

Babycinos

The larger of the two little girls, perhaps five years old, was wheeling a small scooter which the younger child was trying to wrest back.

'The reason I'm helping you,' she said, 'is because you hurt yourself and I want to thank you for hurting yourself because now we get babycinos.'

Parenthood

'Stay out of the puddle,' said his father, but one cannot stay out of a place one is already in.

Everybody Already Knows Everything

'When you smash your skull,' Damon said, as they passed the surgery on the corner of Coleridge and Milton streets, the one their parents took them to when they caught temperatures, rashes or what Dad called 'distemper', the one with stacks of *Reader's Digest*s in each corner of the waiting room, 'When you smash your skull,' he repeated, 'you get a brain bleed and blood goes into your brain.'

'Yeah, that happened to me the first time I cracked open my head,' said Thomas.

The Chinese Meal, Uneaten

The meal I did not eat comprised chicken fried with onions and a few cashew nuts tinged unevenly with soy. This occupied two-thirds of the plate, the remaining one-hundred-and-twenty-degree segment taken up by white rice. Someone behind the curtain dividing dining area from kitchen had perhaps measured this with a protractor. The plate itself sat between cuprous spoon and fork as my then wife and I were, by any glancing judgement, not chopsticks people. To the fork's left, a bread plate was surmounted by four small isosceles triangles of white bread, so smothered in margarine that the only foreseeable purpose to which the faux-bronze butter knife could be put was to engineer its removal.

'Triangular,' I commented.

'I don't know why you chose Chinese,' complained my wife. 'Have you ever liked a Chinese meal in your life?'

The meal my then wife did not eat was the Chef's Special, Mongolian Lamb. I'm guessing that it was about as Mongolian as my wife was, with her fourth-generation Australian whine. Her fried rice certainly appeared to be rice, but considering the quantity of oil still adhering to it in little beads, one might be confused as to whether the frying process had already taken place or whether the table was a stop-off point on the way to the pan.

'Yes, I have.' I was feeling combative – she brought this out in me – even though she was almost certainly correct. I thought I could recall three other meals in different restaurants in towns along the Hume Highway, which despite being the main route between Melbourne and Sydney and about five hundred and fifty miles long, was in those days mostly a single lane in each direction and was not famous for its cuisine. I could not recall enjoying any. My memories of the three meals, if there were indeed three, had fused together into a glutinous compound of rice, cornflour and a pale orange-brown substance which was almost certainly not dilute tea.

'Name one Chinese restaurant on Earth where you've enjoyed a single mouthful.' The problem with my wife, as I knew at some level from the moment we became engaged, was that she could never disengage. At that time nor could I. Her hissing attracted a look or two from the other patrons – a couple at the table next to us and another couple across the room, early diners hoping to clock up a few more miles before checking in to the next cardboard-walled, substandard motel (if heading south) or arriving home (if on the same northerly trajectory as we were).

'That one in Gundagai was good,' I said. 'What was it called? The Lantern or something.'

'Rubbish,' she whispered, as loudly as possible.

'You don't have to eat it,' I said. 'We could leave everything and walk across to the pub. The pub looks fine.

Just the way you like it. Solid as Australia. Regular as the public service. I read the menu last time.'

She poked at a small strip of lamb with the tip of her spoon. Whenever in an ethnic restaurant, it was our practice to doubt the provenance and more particularly the species of the meat. This dated back to a tour group holiday we'd taken three years earlier, in which we'd spent a small amount of time in the company of a meat inspector from Darwin.

'What do you think this is?' she asked, in a tone which could almost have suggested a riddle.

'Meat,' I said.

'Aren't we all?'

The problem with my then wife was bluntness and aggressive passivity that would make a cliff seem friendly, from top or bottom. And stubbornness. She sat there without eating and without rising.

Problems, problems. The problem with me, according to my wife, her family and her allies, was indolence. The problem with indolence was that it had resulted in my lacking employment, a condition which limited my capacity to spend my money on her as all the money we possessed (by process of elimination of the non-earner) was hers.

'Would you like me to shout you a pub dinner too? And after that maybe some Italian? If that doesn't work, who knows what we could find: Greek? Fijian? Icelandic?' asked my wife. 'We could order and abandon meals at every restaurant in town. I'll just phone my parents and ask for an advance on my inheritance.'

I'd heard this once or twice before and bit my lip rather than suggest that if one were actually to kill her parents there would be no need for a forward payment. I guessed she would not find this funny. My wife's parents were not appropriate material for jokes. Her father made clear his dislike of me each time we met, and not so subtly. The employment section of the paper was always open on the table. Lately I had noticed a further downgrade, in that the Casual Work section was now highlighted. He had an inimitable manner.

My wife's mother simply ignored me, or addressed me through her daughter: 'Would he like a cup of coffee? Did he sleep badly?'

The hypothesis came to me that my wife had deliberately brought her parents into the conversation to ensure I lost my appetite completely. I studied the food and concluded that it made no difference.

'So eat up then,' I said, 'and stop complaining.'

Amidst the clumped rice and drying chicken on my plate the cashews glistered like cartoon smiles in the weak lantern light. It was all about as appetising as the thought of our lives together stretching into the future.

A family of four entered the restaurant with a tinkling of the bells tied to the back of the door. The children were already complaining about the food. I could hear the older one rasping away, 'Why do we have to have *Chinese* Australian food? Why can't we just have *Australian* Australian food?'

The mother was responding with ineffective, gritted-teeth patience, 'It means they've got Chinese *and* Australian food both.'

Wait till they saw it! *Mu-um, this is neither. This isn't food at all.* My sour face must have brought the waiter, who had directed the newcomers to a table well away from us and nearer to another couple, still waiting for their meals, and now wearing distressed expressions.

'Everything okay?' the waiter asked.

My wife had already started calling him Peter, as he was labelled in black Dymo tape.

'Fine thanks,' I said, despite this being not the case.

'To be honest not so good, Peter,' said my wife.

Peter stopped. 'The lamb?'

'The lamb's foul and the chicken, well at least I didn't order the chicken,' she said, 'but he is much, much worse.'

'He?'

She'd done it perfectly: poor Peter was stuck between the impulse to turn around and attend and that to run away. The sight brought to life a memory of university, where I'd limped my way through a term of Jean-Paul Sartre's thinking before dropping out (if shallow limping is philosophically conceivable). Sartre had been inspired to characterise the waiter-*qua*-waiter as the epitome of living in bad faith – role-playing obsequiousness, exaggerated formality, ostentation. Observing Peter's response to my wife's faux-honesty, I doubted Sartre had been musing on these most human behaviours in a Chinese restaurant. The fluent nastiness with which my wife had pinned this waiter: it was quite brilliant (brilliant, that is, other than using me as the lever for her trap) and Peter's face lost its waiterish composure immediately.

'Yes,' she continued. 'He's lazy, rude and he never learns from his previous errors and misjudgements.'

'Stop it,' I told her. 'This is unnecessary. Don't pay any attention to her, waiter.'

'I'm very sorry to you both. One moment please.' Peter turned and almost ran back behind the tasselled curtain. I wasn't sure where he'd scooted off to – to resign, effective immediately? Out back to reattach his waiter persona? Back to his books to ink a quick critique of existentialism?

'That wasn't very nice of you,' I said. 'You've upset him.'

'Ha! It's always nice to introduce a little honest intercourse here and there.'

'No. It's not always nice at all. Let's just go. I'm going,' I told her. 'You coming with me?'

'We'll have to agree to disagree on this. I'm not finished eating yet,' she said, picking up her fork and prodding a single tine half-heartedly at the lamb.

'You haven't started.'

I hadn't moved either. We had one car parked outside and a hundred and twenty miles to our destination. I could have left her there, abandoned with nothing to sustain her but coloured cornflour; or I could have dropped the keys on the table, stormed out and caught a train to somewhere, picturing myself with the cold glass of the train windows and the stink of steel friction in the carriage, an olfactory undertone to the cigarette smoke. I could have ended our marriage there and then, a thought which occasionally recurred during our years together after that moment. If only I had left her back then, in that Chinese restaurant, what a life I would have lived! But at that moment I did not have the foresight or the purposefulness and I did not move.

Nobody ate.

Peter returned with a thin perspiring man in a stained white apron.

'This is Alfred,' said Peter. 'You tell him what you want. He's the boss.'

'He tells me you're not happy,' said Alfred. 'How can I help you?'

'It's all okay,' I said (diner-*qua*-diner).

'Look at this lamb,' said my wife, sawing rapidly and ineffectively at it with the side of her spoon. 'Very tough.'

'Bring the lady a knife,' said Alfred, as though he were compelled to speak commandingly. Peter, who had been half-hovering, half-hiding behind Alfred, looked relieved to be sent away from us again. He disappeared back into the kitchen.

'And look at him,' she said, pointing at me with her spoon tip. 'He's my husband, you know, and just look at him.'

I feared she would say more, describe the shame I brought to her family or list my various failures and shortcomings, but Alfred didn't give her the chance.

'He, I cannot help you with,' he said.

A guest at the next table chose that moment to wave his own spoon, 'Excuse me, excuse me. When you have a moment, mate. This soup is not hot.'

'You shouldn't have ordered vichyssoise, old-timer,' commented my wife for my benefit, *sotto voce*. After her non-specific venting about me to Alfred, my wife seemed to settle into a quieter bitterness. The man and woman at the other table were not in fact old. They were about our age, and my wife must have forgotten that we had also aged. Alfred had taken up one of the soup bowls and was holding it with both hands cupped, presumably to assess its temperature.

Peter meanwhile was negotiating unsuccessfully with the newcomers. The two children had already crossed the room once more and stood at the door.

'Let's go, let's go,' called the larger of the two, who might have been six or seven. The smaller one, who was at most three years old, turned it into a chant, 'Le-et's go! Le-et's go,' until the father pulled open the door with some more tinkling and an exaggerated apologetic wave, and they were gone.

Alfred was still holding the small soup bowl. I turned halfway around to look at the neighbours' meals. The soup must have been a side dish, as there was also a plate in front of each of them and a tub of rice. They had no bread and butter. Had they asked for authentic food? If so, it looked disappointing. The meals the couple weren't eating were something like prawns with carrots and beans for her and, for him, a brown gelatinous gloop that I took to be beef with black bean sauce. They had been given both western cutlery and chopsticks.

The woman was holding a single chopstick. I must have fixed on this more intently than I was aware of, for she stopped picking at a carrot with it and stared straight back at me.

'Why don't you take a damned photograph. It'll last longer,' she muttered.

'No damned camera,' I said.

'Shhh,' said my wife, which was a bit rich considering her contribution to our enjoyment of the evening up to that point.

'Too late,' I told her. The man stood up. He was about my height though perhaps chunkier, broad in that manner which makes it difficult to tell whether he was strong or just fat.

'Listen here,' he commenced, wagging a thick finger in my direction.

'Siddown, boofhead,' I said.

'Please,' said Alfred. 'Gentlemen.'

'You keep a civil tongue, mate. I won't have you talking to my wife,' the other man grumbled. His posture was threatening to bring him forward, but he stayed where he stood and, after a further two or three seconds of gesturing, he did as I'd suggested.

'Thank you,' said Alfred. If anything, he was even sweatier than he had been, positively diaphoretic.

'What a pair of dickheads,' said my wife.

'Yep,' said the carrot-eater.

'You're no better,' said my wife. 'You actually started it.'

I estimated the number of additional friends she would make by the end of our meal at zero. I did not estimate the length of the meal.

Carrot-eater swore. My wife gave three claps of applause.

'Listen,' said Alfred. 'You must stop these bad manners or you must leave.'

'Bad manners is the only aspect of this place keeping us here. Otherwise the attractions are pretty limited,' said Carrot-eater. I laughed for the first time that evening.

Alfred scowled briefly, but controlled his expression and switched to a concerned smile.

Peter returned with a knife for my wife. He crossed to the family's abandoned table and removed the tablecloth, making himself very, very busy away from my wife's potential speeches. The four plates of food sat untouched in their places, looking less and less like the photographs in the restaurant window. The only reason my wife stayed put was that I had suggested leaving. Perhaps the other couple stayed so as not to appear to yield the restaurant to us. Interesting how Anglos think of the Chinese as being the ones obsessed with losing face. For a moment I considered explaining this to all present.

'I will bring you new soup,' Alfred offered the other couple and, turning to us, still with his fixed smile, 'but you, I won't offer you anything, the way you make trouble for everyone. You stay or you go, it's up to you, but no more arguing.'

He wiped his forehead with his sleeve, inelegantly took up the soup bowls and exited behind the curtain.

'I wasn't clear on that. Did that include arguing with each other?' I asked my wife.

'Scene two,' said my wife. 'Later the same evening in the same bloody restaurant. All are silent.'

'Scene three,' I said, 'in which someone spills sweet and sour sauce and someone else cleans it up.'

'Shut up, will you,' said Carrot, *a propos*, as they say, of nothing. Her nuggety husband glared at me, ready to leap to her defence in case I might be tempted to respond.

'You see that?' I said to my wife. 'You see that? That's a solid relationship.'

'Just ignore them,' said Nugget, taking up his chopsticks. I realised he was no more skilled with chopsticks than I was: he attempted to pick up a bean but it dropped onto the tablecloth.

My wife waggled her head childishly and repeated, 'Just ignore them.'

'Why didn't we get chopsticks?' I whispered.

'And don't whisper.'

Nugget gave up on the chopsticks and folded his arms. Alfred, now luminescent with dampness, returned with two soup bowls. The couple across the room were attempting to attract Alfred's attention: their food had not yet arrived. Each had an arm in the air. Alfred set down the soup on Carrot and Nugget's table, where the bowls sat steaming and untouched. After an interminable pause, the steam ceased. Peter peered out from the kitchen every now and then, in case something had changed. Perhaps he was hoping the restaurant would have emptied. We stayed, my then wife and I, preparing to sleep, to lay down our heads amidst the dishes and cutlery, our neighbours in their moods, the lace curtains against the front window shifting with each inexplicable draught.

It's Not That

It's not that we had a choice about the point of entry, as every grumpy kid is bound to tell every grumpy parent. Thanks Mum, kind of thanks Dad, said a teenager in a teenaged fashion. Teenaged fashion meaning: grunting and sarcasto. Content meaning: *as if.*

It's not that she thought her life was dynamic and that the lives of others should be static, or that it followed from her sense of others in the world that those others would stay where she left them until she returned. Ha! Good luck with that idea, even if she *had* thought it. It's not that he was at all judgemental, not nearly as much as many are. He considered his life in the same way as she did or didn't consider hers, that he was the dynamo and that others were furniture. This, though, was hardly their primary site of conflictual agreement.

It's not that one should be narrating stories in such a manner. He said and she thought. She said and he thought. Said and said, thought and thought. Blue shift on approach. Red shift on reproach. It's annoying to have to guess who the characters are, complained Georgina. And where, and stuff like that. Just give them all names and set it maybe in a city. *Nyeeeeeeowwww,* dopplered a kid.

What's your name, kid? enquired a passerby.

None of your beeswax, said the kid.

It's not that people don't have the right to decide what they do or don't think about, is it? Think about it, said my mum. No, said the kid (me). I want you to have a good long think about what you did, said an adult. I already thought about it really fast, said a different kid. Some words were on a billboard and some others on a door. And so on. What's your point, said the teenager. You want me to grow up and be an arsehole and get divorced like all adults?

It's not that they all lose their tempers in different ways, shouters and seethers, broadcasters and sulkers, pop-eyes and pouters and shakers and souses. Don't forget the receivers, said a radio. Post-conflict ratio of insomniacs to hibernators is not known, said a policy wonk with a policy wink, and that really set them off.

It's not that half a billion people want to have pointless arguments with people they don't know about ideas they don't understand, is it? It's not that, at a certain moment, a star literally blinked out. (*Literally*, someone must have said or else the word wouldn't have landed right here on the page.) If stars are infinite in number, it makes no theoretical difference to the amount of light in the universe if one twinkles itself to extinction. Otherwise, it makes some. If the extinguishment had occurred in your part of infinity, you would have noticed the diminution, commented someone (not a meteorologist). John, if that was the character's name, cried. About something other than stars. Like, for instance, arguments that may have some point.

It's not that John was hoping someone would place a hand on his shoulder and squeeze. Tiny nerves and capillaries did their things if that happened. He patted at the hand. The hand squeezed. In retrospect, he reconsidered what his hopes of a someone might have been. The hand stayed for a while, and perhaps wasn't sure how to let go.

It's not that characters died in every story Emilia read, and that this caused her despair to grow year by year, so that she had taken it upon herself to save people wherever she sensed grief. Some of the old men on the street just wanted the money, though some also wanted conversation. I haven't been to the movies for eight years, said perhaps Philip or Dilip, but of course that's not why I want fourteen or sixteen dollars. Why is he even there in a sleeping bag, said a kid (different kid). Think about it, said Emilia, more to herself.

It's not that if you were my ex-husband I would try not to shout at you and slam doors every time you came by to collect the kid. It's not that the older I become the more inclined I am to say what I think, to tell the truth, to let diplomacy hit the concrete and shatter into little mannerisms, to fail to account for the feelings you endlessly explain to me. They were trying to nod slowly, but they nodded at the normal pace. You have no idea what normal is, accused a teenager who had not seen daylight in like forever.

It's not that he was not capricious on occasion. It's not that she was afraid of superficiality. It's not that he wasn't who he said he wasn't. It's not that either of them was susceptible to vengeful impulses. Or not only that. Let me tell you who I am and how I'd like to be treated, said a voice.

Someone was shouting something which sounded from where she stood like something else. That's too unhelpful, said Georgina's friend, in the comments. The fuck would you know, said several other commenters. Bitch.

It's not that materialism is a new phenomenon. Things were once made from stone, which in general meant they were extremely durable, proponed Alex. People liked having those things, in all likelihood, though many were not very transportable. You can't say 'in all likelihood' as an unsupported filler, said a kid (prodigious) who wasn't there. She and he thought different things in relation to the same stimulus, but only discovered this later when they had to converse. It's not that thinking was the problem. Should you define who Alex is? queried an editor in a margin note.

It's not that one can finesse contentment. Various people calling out 'Don't even try' and 'Don't risk it' and 'Oh my goodness'. (People in this audience are as polite as can be, considering all the heckling.) John, feeling encouraged, has by now stopped crying. No one has judged him except for one professional in a small room. Happy now? said a narrator to another implied character, who shook her head and pouted like a selfie. It's not that probability couldn't apply, she said, but that it doesn't apply. All the intellectuals made jokes which we all got, including me.

It's not that anyone reads anymore, not in the immersed manner of the good old days, said someone of a certain type. Georgina's friend went apoplectic in the comments. All of the youths went feral, once per generation. The leadership went AWOL. I went already, whined a little kid. I went like *blam*, lied a teenager with gunfingers. Considering everything, that went as well as could be expected. *Unexpected*, corrected one of the parties to the dispute, went as well as could be *un*expected. Time we went back to the main story, said a kid. Whatever that's supposed to mean, went one of the teenagers from before the story began.

It's not that people grow apart, said a man on TV, because people are not that much like forks in trees. A bunch of people I don't know were nodding. The kid had grown, not really taller or wider, but kind of grown to suit the house. Gothic or colonial? joked the relative who makes those jokes. Obviously the kid was mopey, being a kid. She said a whole bunch of stuff that she'd been saving up since March, just stopped biting her lip and released it all at once. Had he said something to provoke or even to provide an opening? He'd been Mr Low Profile around the house and Mr Projectile in his mind. That's what point of view is all about, replied Georgina to her friend. I don't know, said her friend for the first time, because up till then she'd always known everything. It would be better if there were maybe three or four kids, she said, by way of recovery.

It's not that there was a moment when you could or couldn't say goodbye. He had something wrong with his ear. She had exams. The kid was filling more and more of the house, but not because of growing. Maybe there was another kid as well, a bit smaller but similar looks, so that two or three rooms were always kid-occupied. Plus a teenager overflowing with atmospherics. It's not that that cleaved them together or apart. It's not that John pre-enacted what was about to happen with the two of them. It's not that there was a deadline for everything except goodbye. It's not that everything kind of blurred into their lives. The blurriness somehow seemed to come out of their eyes.

It's not that endings are so distinguishable from beginnings. It's not that we are snakes following or swallowing our tails or tales. It's not that cyclical and circular mean the same. Everyone needs to know what state they find themselves in, psychocorporeally and geographically, generalised the well-defended Chris, whom I don't remember meeting. I don't know how I feel, even when I reflect very deeply or at length on myself, said a vessel or vehicle. The kid grew a bit more. The other kid or kids, probably as well, but no evidence. True that someone or other was tired, more tired than usual, but it isn't that anyone was worn down. It's not that.

It's something else.

The Tin Can Story

My brother rang me the other day as I was driving across town. He had just moved house; I figured perhaps he was about to ask me to dinner, which would in ordinary circumstances have been a rare occurrence, and he did offer an invitation of sorts. He wanted to know whether, seeing as how I didn't have a proper job, I would wait there the following morning. Some kind of issue with the pipes needed attending to, and the plumber was due at 9.30.

Thanks very much. I could have pointed out that having a range of freelance engagements was actually a job, and that I was frequently extremely productive. No doubt he would have expressed agreement and denied that he had implied anything other than that I might be free for an hour or two on a particular morning. Had he said I was unproductive? Had he stated that regular employment hours were preferable to occasional paid engagements? He knew that I was happy with my choice of employment lifestyle.

In return I could have noted to my brother that every conversation with him had embedded within it some kind of a reminder of his earning capacity compared with mine – nonsense, didn't I recognise that he had a senior role and it went without saying that he would be appropriately rewarded just as my work had its own rewards – but as usual I said nothing of the sort, agreed to his request and undertook to be at his house by 9.15 at the latest so as to make sure I would be there on time because plumbers don't wait around if you're late, and their time is valuable. Surely I wasn't over-reading the implication in this about my own time? He repeated the address, which he was disappointed to hear I hadn't remembered from the real estate link he'd sent seven weeks earlier. I had to hang up any moment, I told him. The connection was not so good as I was driving through the city and had to go into a tightly scheduled meeting very, very soon, as soon as I had found an unmetered parking spot, and there were many tall buildings and overhead wires.

Oh yeah, the key – he would leave the key in a tin on the front veranda.

Bye.

Bye.

Although I'm not always known for punctuality, I arrived with plenty of time to find two tins sitting there on the veranda. In these situations I sometimes play a sort of luck game with myself – if I could pick the correct tin, I'd be in for a good day. Left or right? Would he leave it further from the door (more secure) or nearer (the ol' double bluff)? Guessed he'd play it straight. And *yesss*: my first choice of tin held a key.

Maybe my brother had double-doubled – regarding security methods and bluffs, just how strategic was he? This brass key wouldn't turn in the brass keyhole. Second tin, second key? *Nope*. The other tin was empty. I had been right. Logic and understanding of the human mind are two of my strengths. Therefore: one key, another door. I made my way down the side of the house. There had been no talk of back doors, I was almost sure. Through the glass sliding door I could see his newly purchased though unrenovated kitchen. The brass key didn't fit this lock either – aluminium fitting, so not even a likely match – or perhaps it was a duplicate key and hadn't been filed properly. Or checked. By him.

The back door, though, was not locked. The house move must not be suiting my brother's temperament, for him to overlook this. I slid the door open, stepped through and sat at the kitchen table to fiddle with my phone and wait. My brother's laminated kitchen table must have deteriorated in the move, and was piled with plates and saucepans. Seemed as though his sense of order had deteriorated in the move too – that thought gave me unedifying satisfaction. My phone, on the other hand, had no satisfaction to offer. No emails had arrived. It was not my turn in any games. No one had interacted with any of my social media profiles.

A weird gurgly, growly sound commenced somewhere further into the house. Intermittent and extremely annoying, this must be what prompted the call for the plumber. I stood and deposited the phone back in my pocket. What to do? Explore the house? Attend to the noise somehow? I had once bent a wire thingo inside the toilet cistern and this initiative had stopped a much milder hissy sound, but my plumbing skills were otherwise unrenowned. So forget it. Let him pay the plumber for piping.

I sat down for a moment and stood up again. What to do in an unfamiliar house. Go through his stuff? Shuffle the paperwork? I was here to do my brother a favour, so these intrusive thoughts ought to be suppressed.

The fridge. That ought to provide a distraction. I wondered if my photo was on his fridge. After all, I was the person he turned to when someone was needed to sit in a house for a morning. But there were no family pics at all – the fridge exterior was bare other than a couple of photos of acrobats clipped from a magazine, perhaps by my niece. One showed a trapeze artist, just released, smiling towards the camera; the second, two sequined women gesticulating in conversation, each balanced on the shoulders of a sequined man. Funny little thing, my niece.

Standing before the fridge reminded me that I hadn't eaten breakfast. I opened the fridge and lifted out a bottle of green juice, took a couple of swigs and replaced it. Toast might be the thing, but where was the bread?

Growling of pipes ceased for a moment and was replaced by scratching. That surely can't have been the plumbing. Rats – they were infested with rats. Ooh boy, he wouldn't like that at all. I thought to leave him a note about it. He knew I'd previously had a rat issue, and occasionally referred to it when a context could be extended to contain rodentism, such as any mention of Norway or feral mammals. Given my experience and therefore acquired expertise, I reasoned that he might appreciate a recommendation for pest exterminators. I couldn't see a notepad anywhere – this was something I'd have expected to see magnetised to his fridge. I tore off a strip of newspaper from the pile on the table and searched for a pen. The scratching stopped. For a moment there was silence. I checked my phone: 9.53. Where was this plumber? I should have asked for a contact number, or my brother should have thought to have provided it.

Perhaps I could fix it after all, and get out of there. I picked my way along the hallway past a couple of piles of removalist's boxes. The growling sound had restarted, but was now more of a quiet wailing. The scratching sounded more desperate than ever, and all the noise seemed to emanate from the bathroom door. I reached for the handle. As I gripped it, ready to twist it, a sudden thump hit. I jumped back. A single nail came straight through the door, very close to the handle. I thought for a second someone had hammered the nail through, which made no sense at all. And the nail was slightly curved, perhaps not metal. I must have frozen for a moment, my hand hovering close to the handle without taking it. The nail disappeared back the way it had come.

At that very moment, I heard the plumber on the front veranda. Thank God! I withdrew my hand and backtracked around via the kitchen and veered left across the living room towards the front.

Disquietingly, as I reached the front door the plumber pushed a key into the lock and was jiggling it this way and that. The door swung open. The plumber stood before me, wearing a long red coat and a top hat, and carrying a leather barbecue tool of some description. He looked more surprised than I felt.

'What the coathook are you doing in my house?' he said.

'Why do you have a key to my brother's house?' I retorted. 'Are you here to fix the plumbing or not?'

The barbecue tool unravelled to reveal a horsewhip.

'Whoa, whoa,' I said. 'Just give me a moment.'

I was showing him my hands, in one of which I held my phone.

'Just ringing my brother.' I probably say 'just' a lot when uncomfortable.

'I think you should leave now,' said the plumber.

'Yes, yes,' I said, holding up my hand like a traffic cop's.

'Where the bloody heck are you?' answered my brother. 'The plumber's been waiting half an hour.'

'At your place. And the plumber has just walked in this second wearing a red morning coat.'

'A what?' asked my brother.

'I'm not the plumber,' said the plumber, waving his barbecue-tool-cum-whip this way and that in an increasingly agitated manner.

'And he says he's not the plumber,' I relayed.

'Has he fixed it?'

'He just walked in.'

'This is my home, you imbecile.'

'And he's very rude. Did you know that?'

'No, he's lovely. Are you at 12 Mountain Street?'

'12 Fountain Street, as you said.'

'You are what? I did not!'

I hung up on him. The phone rang immediately, but I ignored it.

'Very sorry,' I said to the not-the-plumber. 'My brother made a mistake with his address.'

'Someone made a mistake. You're very lucky. Did you touch anything?'

'No, I promise.'

'Good.'

I stepped around him and onto the veranda.

'I hope you didn't disturb the leopard,' he said, as I anteloped my way down the path.

Feverish

I went looking for myself and there I was, in a small, darkened room.

You've got to get out of here, I said to myself.

I don't got to do anything, I told myself right back. I was impatient because nothing had worked out at all so far.

Come on, things will be better once you're out. And you'll have the chance to see yourself properly.

Why would that be any better than not seeing myself properly or seeing myself improperly?

We're our own worst enemy.

Kind of.

What?

There are several alternative enemies, so enemies but not worst.

Aah. You coming?

Not sure.

What do you think the outcome will be here?

We'll do our best to stay alive.

Yes, either way.

Noiseless

Disgorged out of that lawyer's office onto the blinking street, Simeon applied the noise-cancelling headphones *sforzando* to his head. Something better fucking work around here, seeing as he'd just been the least effective fucking noise producer in the history of sound. He adjusted the headband – will these headphones cancel the words he had heard ten minutes previously? Well, will they? Fuck that lawyer. Fuck his oleaginous presentation. Fuck the fucking documentation. Simeon was standing still outside the narrow doorway. A bus lodged its scream into his parietal lobe, where the sound persisted a few bars longer than seemed possible. It shouldn't have even got in there. Fuck that too. Simeon slapped the left-side earpad or earpiece or whatever it was called, but it didn't cancel the world out – the bus shouted some gears at him and fucked off. Fuck. The fucking things had cost him two hundred and fifty dollars so should do their advertised job. Under-promise and over-deliver – or, if you were a fucking lawyer, receive promise, agree to it, steal fucking everything. He fiddled with the phone, pressing the Play/Pause button repeatedly. This too was a design fault as there should have been separate buttons. Or *regions*. Of course it was not a real button, just a set of screen coordinates some geeky kid had come up with. BUT WHO FUCKING CARES?

He wrenched them off. For a moment, he might have thrown the whole assemblage onto the ground and stomped off. Somehow he stopped himself without the fury subsiding. Better to have thrown the lawyer onto the ground and stomped off – or stomped *on* the fucker, come to think of it – after the not-quite-apologetic crap the smarmy old fart had subjected him to. But he also knew it was right not to have done it, he didn't need to be arrested on top of ripped off.

The lawyer. He performed lawyerness with his entire being. Did he ever step out of it? Was he a lawyer when he got home to his studio-photographed children or his twenty-megapixel wife? Fuck.

That's the way the cookie crumbles, *so*, un*for*tunately, the lawyer had said in his over-articulated trochees, or perhaps he'd added a further condescending frame: That, my boy, is un*for*tunately the way et cetera. And followed it with further infuriating fake mollification: Though the cards might have fallen another way and given a different result, but we mere humans can't argue with the forces of fate. Smile. Like a parody lawyer, what's it called, the supercession of simulacra. Do actual lawyers actually exist anymore? Or only a kind of lawyer-shaped space emitting platitudes instead of cosmic signals. *Smile*. The lawyer's name persisted on a card in the angry man's pocket. For a few moments it was no longer in his memory, from which Simeon had cancelled it by force of will, but the erasure was somehow undone and the lawyer's presence reasserted itself, that self-parodying image of lawyerness quoting Aristotle, 'The wise man bears the accidents of life with dignity and grace, making the best of his circumstances.' Smarmy smile. *Smarle*.

Shit fuck. Fuck shit.

No need for that, son. (Did he actually say 'son'? Surely Simeon's memory was embroidering – a stitch-up – but the recollection was lodged in his head.) I'm sorry for you. Once things have come to this they cannot be undone, the lawyer smiled, would that smile never be wiped? Simeon had felt his shoulders tense and his fists clench. He smiled too, a forced mirroring, with the thought of cancelling the fucking lawyer's nose. He set his mouth and looked the lawyer in those yellowed Anglo-Saxon eyes. The lawyer blanched, seeing in return the flare in Simeon's eyes, or imagining it. Simeon shifted slightly. We're both dead if he steps forward, the lawyer thought, me first. One dead and white, the other dead and red. There was the button under his desk and he felt for it. Simeon wasn't that big – he wasn't, as it is said, *built* – but the lawyer added the certifiable fury in Simeon's expression to the documentable facts that he looked taut and he looked up for trouble, and let the record show that his fists were so tight it was possible they could not be undone. The lawyer pressed his palm against the underside of the desk, three fingers now against the smooth curve of the button, but he didn't press. Affidavit-ready but no affidavit. Okay. Self-control all around.

Simeon subsided and watched the lawyer, whatever his fucking name was, ease back into his chair. Duress button, divined Simeon. Ha. Fucking shit. I might not have a total grip of myself, not always, but I can play him like a puppet, here we go, ha, now lean forward, hold there, one-two-three, and now relax. I can play him like a fucking ballet school. Bubble up, bubble up, you great empty sack, sink back now. Simeon loomed towards him slightly and saw the lawyer's hand twitch forward again. Come on, show me your incisors again, is that a smile or saffron moonrise over the chinless night? In-out-in-out, rocked Simeon, timing it, syncopating the fucker. Ha fucking ha. Simeon rolled out a thinking face to prolong the sport. No one was saying anything – presumably the lawyer was charging someone by the increment. Eventually they played themselves out: Simeon switched back to fury-face and the amnesia-inducing lawyer said, Well if there's nothing else. Fuck that, Simeon said, there's plenty and you'll be hearing, but they both already knew no one would hear anything, and Simeon slammed his fist on the desk for the hell of it and stomped down the stairs and onto M Street, turned left, stomped a further fifty metres and let out a yell that had pedestrians near him backing away.

There in the street Simeon danced a couple of left jabs and a right uppercut. Are you English? Couldn't you get a job in England? Did your accent precede or post-date the yellowness of your teeth?

It was twilight out there by now, and a nearly full real moon emerged like a lawyer's faked astonishment. Simeon considered telling someone what had happened and how the fuckers had ripped him off. There had been informal undertakings, gentlemen's agreements. But who could he complain to as he'd fallen out with everyone he could think of, everyone who had once been trustworthy? Cut out of this and everything else since forever, and such potential all gone up, that's life but you wouldn't expect it from family.

Don't get paranoid here, he told himself. Don't go building conspiracies from two people having similar stupid ideas. No need to assume a pancake just because someone says flour and someone says eggs. Breathe nicely. Everything that happens is just one thing.

Yeah right. The world was full of people who didn't believe that one. If flour and eggs meet up in a bowl, that's not by chance. Life is the cumulative effect of intention as well as fortune.

But anyway. He had to talk himself down, no good had come of shouting at Yellowtooth. Simeon had finally worked the headphones into the right position – curiously, he sarcasted to himself, it had taken finesse rather than force. This lawyer encounter went to demonstrate something, like maybe don't get your hopes up just because someone swore themselves blue that they weren't going to let you down, and number two on top of that, the problem of relying on yourself when you're hopeless. Simeon felt the tension building again as he cycled through blaming others and self-blame. He went through in his mind everything which might have in the past calmed him, images from here and there in those childhood moments when he wasn't completely miserable: sitting in a tree when a bird landed, swimming in a wave with a school of fish, walking somewhere unfamiliar and seeing a puppy. It took him about half a second to recognise the pattern – somewhere bland seeing something fluffy – and for that sense of self-loathing to grab his throat. Walking along this footpath now seemed a mistake. He should have come down those stairs from the lawyer's office and kept on descending, he should have sunk into the ground. He was just walking, not going home or anywhere. He was too angry to notice his own grief. Either way. Jab–jab. Haymaker.

Some stranger said, Whoa mate, you going okay there? Simeon dropped his hands, took a few quick steps, looked up.

He'd somehow arrived in a familiar part of town, where he had been often a decade or two earlier. Hung out. He was conscious of his age. The city was crowded with fantastically beautiful young people as though for deliberate contrast with the sense of his own decrepitude. His head didn't feel right. He couldn't remember the walk here. How much time had the fucking lawyer caused to disappear?

Eat. Food. Drink. Poison. He should chew off his own arm. Fifty more metres. Pub. He followed a foully content couple through the door, adhering to some principle of aerodynamics, and found himself a place at the adjacent table. He pulled off the headphones. Whoa, noisy as fuck. Did someone say something? Did everyone?

What? Simeon said. *What?*

The couple ignored him, which was steadfast and easy as why the fuck would he be speaking to them rather than into the fucking air. A waitress came over and said to him, Are you going to order something because otherwise the table. He said, Yeah yeah, bring me something and shoved a credit card at her, which wasn't how things worked here. Drinks at the counter and menu on that board up there, she said. She won the rudeness comp because of her competence. He was just winging it.

He left the satchel on the table, What else can anyone take from me, ordered a beer. None of the brands seemed familiar. An ordinary beer, he said to the unsmiling, too-lovely-to-exist barperson. Okay. To eat? To drink, Simeon said, as repayment for no smile. No need to be that, said the vision, who Simeon realised was a bit blurry round the edges, and what was that all about?

And also

Red and blue came over the bar in a great sweep. He pulled money from his pocket and handed over a note without looking at its value. His lips, something strange about them. He pressed his hands against the bar. She pushed some change towards him, but he didn't manage to take it. Strange angles. He heard her say something. Hey mate, what are you doing? Maybe she said something else. You okay? It seemed in context but who could tell. He couldn't look at her or at anything. The lip feeling covered his face and neck. He found the beer and turned towards his table. The couple he'd followed in were tragic pillars of salt backlit by the desert. Simeon reached towards them and watched the beer arc ahead of him in the direction of their table. He felt, for an instant, his shoulder against her arm, and his chin hit the table, which might have hurt.

But didn't.

That phase of his life ended.

He was looking up into some lights, which hurt. A man's voice was saying Mate-mate-mate or something. He tried to open his mouth. Instead of talk something else was coming out and a repulsed voice said Awwww.

He heard removalists (?) discussing him: Turn him on his side, maybe lift his legs, careful.

He heard someone say Call an ambulance and he was trying to say No, no, I'm actually fine, but he felt himself shifted onto a surface and lifted through the air and he was still trying to say no as someone said, Can you tell me your name, what's your name, someone took his wallet and was saying, Here, it's Simon, is it Simon, Simon? Can you tell me what happened? And the girl's voice was saying, He'd just arrived and didn't seem drunk, just kind of weird and he started crying and then this.

The fuck, said Simeon, strapped down, eyes closed. Let me up.

You've had a fall, said a voice.

I'm not ninety-seven, he thought. He felt himself lifted and realised his eyes were still closed. He opened them, saw the arseholes who'd strapped him down. Plus it was too bright and nausea came up from somewhere below the strapping.

Uh-oh, said Captain Efficiency in full paramedical polish. Sit him up.

Simeon now had his arms, so tried to punch someone. Ineffectual. Fuck.

I don't consent to anything, you fucker, said Simeon. I want my money.

Simon. We'll bring your things. Don't worry.

I'm not Simon.

Mister. Hey, Frank, check his name? Mate, you're a bit of a mess. You going to let us clean you up? You fell and you're a mess. Any allergies? Epilepsy? Has this ever happened before?

Oh, his name's *Simeon*.

Aah. Simeon, any allergies?

Yeah, said Simeon. Lawyers.

The uniforms laughed. A cloth swooped at his face, warm. He let them clean him. Someone stuck something in his ear and withdrew it. A thing gripped his arm and loosened.

Can I give him the shot? said Frank.

Nuh. Chuck it in the sharps. Sign it 'refused'. Mate, we're going to take you in for a check-up, the voice said. The altitude changed.

No, said Simeon, trying to swing his legs around.

You can tell that to the doctors. I have to bring you in, so you may as well relax about it or I'll strap you down again. You been drinking? Taken anything?

No, said Simeon again.

He just got here, said No-Smile, hadn't drunk anything.

Not here, anyway, said the paramedic who wasn't Frank.

Simeon fought like a baby to stay awake, slept and woke and was in motion. After some time, paramedics or removalists parked him in a corridor or narrow room. Someone fastened a cuff around his bicep. Every few minutes it tightened, beeped, loosened.

A nurse handed him a cup of juice.

Fuck, he said, maybe aloud. I stink.

Yep. I'll get that sorted for you in a moment. Is there anyone you would like to contact? Wife, partner, friend, relative? Expected anywhere?

I can't, said Simeon. The fucking thieves stole my money.

You were robbed?

Took everything.

Oh no! That's not what was handed over to me. Pete, you got anything about a robbery? Has he been assaulted?

No. Just something about a lawyer.

Fucking cunt of a lawyer, said Simeon. No response: fucking behaviourist crap.

The nurse continued: You were robbed? (Pause.) Were you hit? (Pause.) Did anyone hit you? (Pause.) Have you a head injury? (Pause.) Okay, did you bump your head? (Pause.) Would you like to report something to the police? I can call them for you.

Oh, for fuck's sake. How much fucking thoroughness do I need in my life? He only thought it, but he thought it intensely. I gotta go, he said instead. He pulled the fucking cuff off. The lawyer.

I wouldn't, said the nurse. Rest first, then decide.

No. He took a couple of steps towards the door and felt the nausea building up inside him. Fuck. Bile in, bile out. The taste of his own halitotic mouth. He sat back on the bed, throat burning.

Good idea, said the nurse.

Not good, rasped Simeon, not at all.

Never mind. Sounds like you've had a shock, but we'll get you cleaned up and you'll feel much better.

Small fucking prophecies. Simeon knew he stank, but once they'd put him in a gown, he'd be fucked.

Clothes, he said. I need clothes.

We'll send them down to laundry. You can have them back first thing.

Now, I'll need them now, said Simeon, but he wasn't even sure if the words had come out audibly. They were circumlocutory bastards, all of them. Doctors, nurses, fucking lawyers.

Pete, can you shower him? said the nurse in what Simeon realised was a true, non-nurse-act voice.

No trouble, said Pete, who looked like he could handle himself should any trouble actually form itself in Simeon's head.

This was worse and worse. Pete drew a couple of disposable gloves from a dispenser on the sill.

Come on, mate, said Pete, unbuttoning the top couple of buttons of Simeon's disgusting shirt. You can do your own trousers, can you?

But I haven't got any other clothes, said Simeon. He sounded very small to himself.

Don't worry, we'll sort you out. But let's get this lot fixed up first.

The lawyer, said Simeon.

Your lawyer's not going anywhere either, said Pete. And I know a thing or two about lawyers.

Simeon found himself naked and sitting on a plastic chair in the shower enclosure. The water came out cold, warmed slightly without ever becoming quite hot enough, but it was better than being covered in crud. He wiped at his face and neck with the sponge Pete handed him. After a couple of minutes he began to shiver. Pete switched off the water and helped him into a hospital robe and tied it at the back.

Fuck, said Simeon out loud. One step below a fucking straitjacket.

He had been compliant as all fuck, just like with the lawyer, same fucking problem as had got him into all this.

At least five steps below, said Pete. And I'd try to tone down the language. That's if you want to get out of here. There's a neurologist coming to have a chat.

What the fuck for? said Simeon, or maybe he didn't, and the robe was sticking to his residual dampness.

Pete had him by the bicep and led him back to the bed, backing him up with just enough force to ensure he sat.

Nothing's going to happen out there in the world that you won't deal with better when you're well, said Pete. Nothing.

I'm fine, said Simeon. What do you think is wrong with me. These fuckers. This isn't fucking *Bleak House*, mate. These bastards aren't going to wait.

Phone them up, said Pete. I've had to deal with lawyers in my life, probably been in more strife than you, or maybe not quite as much, but anyway. The promise of a letter from another solicitor usually pauses them for a while.

A phone call won't do anything, said Simeon.

My response to your letter of the 14th will be with you tomorrow, said Pete. Does that sound credible?

What, said Simeon. What the fuck.

I'm a natural, boasted Pete. Come on, it can't do any harm and it could work. I could write it down for you if you like.

Tell you what, said Simeon. You phone them.

Ha, said Pete. His mouth twisted with half-serious consideration. Ha. All right, I will. Always good to broaden your role. Give us the number then.

Doing something would be better than nothing, that's what Simeon was thinking. Pete dialled the lawyer.

Hello, said Pete. Aah good, you are just the person with whom I was hoping to speak. I'm Peter calling from G and L Solicitors. We've received instructions from our client Mr Simeon Axel with regard to your conversation with him earlier today. (Very long pause. Pete eyebrowed towards Simeon, who raised a thumb in reply.) Our understanding, continued Pete, is that you were quite specific. (Long pause.) Uh-huh. Well, we will be responding to your statements and purported actions within seven days. (Pause.) My client through us will view most unfavourably any further actions you take within those seven days and we will respond accordingly. (Short pause.) Yes, of course. I'll send this through to you in writing tomorrow morning, as my secretary has left for the day. Have you made a note? (Very short pause.) Thank you. Goodbye.

That will delay them, said Pete. So many patients need that kind of assistance it ought to be part of my job. Now, how about you get some rest? Once the neurologist sees you, things will become clearer. Reassurance: better than morphine and less paperwork.

Right. Thanks, said Simeon. He was feeling a kind of apprehensive or conditional gratitude. Or was that a combination of fear and emotional abdication? The tension was still there, but covered up with verbiage.

Still, he must have been to some extent mollified. Simeon allowed himself to be helped into the bed, the heavy coolness of clean sheets, a pillow not quite right, fluorescent lighting flicked off overhead as Pete hit the switch, but still coming through the internal windows.

He closed his eyes, was instantly asleep and dreaming of Pete meeting with the lawyer, bounced back after what felt like two minutes but instead was the middle of the night. Weird time-compression shit. Clock: 3:33AM. He swung his feet over the side of the bed. Someone had placed hospital slippers there. On. He stood up. The corridor was empty and he couldn't decide which way to turn, but what did it matter. Someone groaned from the next room. A bell sounded and a light came on somewhere. Funny how everyone wakes at the same time for no reason. He took a few steps along the corridor. What exactly did he want? Maybe one of those hospital cheese sandwiches. There was no one at the nurses' station and he called out, Hello?

A cross nurse with a question-mark face emerged.

Sandwich, he said.

She gestured towards Patient Kitchen.

A tray of sandwiches sat there on the bench, and he took one. The bread had dried out, but this was in a way comforting, the expectedness of that texture. He put a few of the dry sandwiches onto a saucer and returned to the room, placing them on his tray-table. He pulled the folder from the foot of the bed and flicked through the notes.

Up the top of the page someone had written *assess neuro. cog imp? Fall? Vom and vom times.* In another hand was *Possible aggro Avoid startle.*

Oh great, he thought. But bullshit. I'm a perfect gentleman. Blood pressure and temperature graphs seemed fine enough. There was a drug chart, but a headache tablet was the only thing on it. It seemed to Simeon that he had been given something other than a headache tablet, but what could it have been? He couldn't recall details of when or by whom. Might it have been before he'd fainted, perhaps in the lawyer's office? Simeon couldn't remember if he'd accepted so much as a glass of water from that agent of thieves. He couldn't picture the exchange, so rang for the nurse.

How come the only thing charted is a headache tablet? he asked.

You're quite right, dear, said the same punctuation-faced nurse. I'll write down *sandwich* for you. Did you just have the one?

No …

I'll write two then, shall I?

No. I think someone gave me something, said Simeon, but this sounded unreliable even to him.

Uh-huh. I'll ask around, she said. Is there anything else?

No. No thank you.

Okay, dear. Ring if you need anything.

Simeon struggled to think and fell asleep before he achieved anything like clarity.

Pete woke him by opening the curtains, behind which Simeon could see a dismal fountain of smoke rising from the hospital incinerator. He felt a little better for the sleep.

Do I have time for a quick sauna before check-out? he joked.

You have a couple of scans booked, said Pete, in nurse mode.

Fuck. I don't consent to anything, said Simeon, switching to oppositional defiance. Where are my clothes?

Patience, said Pete. We're all on your side.

I know what that means, said Simeon. I've got to get out of here.

Cooperation will get you out sooner, said Pete. You seem fine to me but you've been charted as *MCI? Release only into care.*

What the fuck's MCI?

Easy on the language. Mild cognitive impairment. All that stuff about the lawyer seems to have been noted as non-sequential and possibly paranoid. Neurologist thinks you banged your head when you fell.

Bullshit, said Simeon. I didn't bang anything. Get me my clothes. I'll walk out fucking naked.

You could, but it wouldn't go too well. I'm officially directed to restrain you to prevent risk of harm to yourself or others. You are an official risk.

What, said Simeon. What fucking bullshit. Let me see it. Who the hell put that out? This is freaking me out.

Never mind, said Pete. I can sort that out for you. You've been charted for sedation on request.

You mean you can treat the anxiety but not the directive? Simeon's face twitched itself.

You got it. Fix the freak-out, leave the law.

No.

Your choice.

Simeon sagged into the bed, or he felt as though he had. What he assumed was breakfast lay hidden under an apricot-coloured plastic cover on a trolley. Apricot-*ish*. The pillow was still wrong.

You should eat something, said Pete. He smiled briefly and wasn't there any more.

Fuck everything and everyone, Simeon said, aloud. He poured himself lukewarm tea, ate a piece of soggy toast, got up.

In a wardrobe in a corner of the Patient Kitchen hung somebody's gabardine coat. He put it on. Slightly large, better than way too small. No one in the corridor. Good. What the hell, he was thinking, enough ridiculousness in the world. Face-mask on a tray in the hallway outside the ward. On it went. Cough-cough for a bit of realism. Hospital slippers, no money, chopped out of the old woman's will because of the lying thief of a son. Fuck him, fuck him. It would not stand. Simeon on the bus without swiping any ticket anywhere, off the bus, into the stale old charity shop on N Street, sob story about clothes stolen in the night. You poor dear, no accusations or bullshit from her, that's how you treat people down on luck. New old trousers and shirt, and life began again. Now, let's talk about lawyers. Let's get some fucking headphones.

In the Time It Takes to Finish a Sandwich, We Could Build Worlds

You and I, my dear sister, you and I, just as we have always been: with my vision and your pragmatism, your receptiveness and my intensity, your catering and my generosity of spirit, my artistry and your critique. I have the sandwich in hand and, with it, trace out my words in the air ...

... and if the idea about the furniture rental system doesn't work out – and unfortunately it's not for the moment in my control but is rather in the purview of those without the expansive, entrepreneurial outlook you and I share, that is, those who follow a set of procedures based on what has worked in the past and not at all considering what will or is likely to work in the future (and I know this because I emailed it through using the official corporate online contact form, attentioned properly to the Innovation Team) – but should it come to pass that at some point the idea about the furniture, or plan, really, more like a plan, *much* beyond an idea, should this not proceed owing to failures of vision or for whatever reason, you may also like my idea, or plan, for the Orchard, which doesn't depend so much on the capacity or incapacity of others but only on the use of a patch of land which is not being used for anything at all and so there is no reason whatsoever why it should not be available to plant a few trees once we've cleared away the weeds that have taken over the site.

At this point, I reel in my free-flowing sandwich and take a bite. As I had been running through the plan or plans, your left-hand index finger had been doing the conversational work for you – tappity tap tappity, allegro nervoso four bars and two bars ritardando, minim rest and a tempo – but now I can see you've been assiduous in your attention, for despite appearances and despite the weird breathiness in the tone as you set out, you ask me where this land is, what access we have to it and what checks, if any, I have made. I've always been the risk-taker and you the risk-averse of us, and now I chew for a while, chewing in the manner that shows that I'll swallow as soon as practicable in order to answer your questions, no matter how constrictive they appear to me. You draw out your sandwich, wrapped in greaseproof paper, from the café-branded bag, carefully fold back a paper edge so as not to lose a strand of whatever those sprouts are called, take a perfect-sized bite.

So if this table is the city, the land is approximately on your left shoulder, far enough away that it has been ignored for all these years – for all eternity as far as I know – except by lantana and bamboo and blackberries and privet which pay attention everywhere at all times, and even if someone does actually own this land, they may be completely unaware of it, so the choice to be made is whether to clear and plant or whether to try and find out who the owner is (the owner in black letter law, that is, if not in practice or in any connected sense), and to offer them some proportion of the proceeds, gross or net, even though this may draw attention to the value of the land and they may try to take over my plan notwithstanding that they wouldn't have even thought of doing anything, and might not have been aware of the land at all, but for us drawing their attention to it, that is, if the land is actually owned by anyone and not just sitting there unowned (even by the black letter of the law), and if that's the case I'm almost certain that the land would become ours (or mine if you decide in your careful way against joining me) after only a very short time, something like three years or maybe seven years – it's called something like ownership through possession, maybe there's an extra adjective that goes in there, not sure, but not that important by comparison to the potential fruit to be taken to market.

A small piece of tomato has slipped from the side of my sandwich onto the plate. I pick it up and pop it into my mouth, and you take this opportunity to fill the atmosphere with negative thinking, further elucidating and elaborating all the blocks to my plan, drawing on your multitudinous yet unbacked boasts to know more about land law and its operation than I do and in immediate subsequence explaining how little I understand of the complexities of providing evidence for and attaining the right to claim land through what you call adverse *possession. When I chew at the sandwich, you bite. You bite at me.*

I'd expected your scepticism as you have always been, of the two of us, the more defensive and the more sceptical – well, different when we were young and when bruises healed faster – but can I just say that nothing, really nothing, depends on any type of claim, inverse or converse, adverse or obverse or transverse, to that or any particular piece of land, so that if we were moved on, or given your hesitation, if *I* were moved on after a few years

81

and before being able to keep the land through any verse or the universe of possession, by that time I or we would have built up plenty of fruit-growing skills and it wouldn't matter if we needed to shift – *plus* I'm very confident we'll have saved up enough to purchase our own Orchard, even if we sold only, say, twenty kilograms of fruit per day, just a couple of boxes for, say, fifty or seventy dollars per box, you can see how that would all add up – the object is not to get something for nothing, some cargo cult variation, but simply to turn a good idea into a good and satisfying life, and can I say it grieves me that you, rather than embracing what could be, instead turn your mind to fault-picking and hole-finding, but no matter.

And what are sandwiches for other than biting and punctuation? I pierce the doubled bread and you pierce my soliloquy. You, somewhat submerged, swim for the surface, and you're spluttering, I think, or so it seems, with a desire to simultaneously reassure and deflate, that of course you mean nothing but good for me, and that your desire to chip away at any ideas or plans I have been thinking about and developing over days, or weeks, your desire is only that I find fulfilment and a measure of success.

Thank you, of course, for recognising that such ideas don't just fall out of sleeves but are matters of great consideration, but if lands and Orchards fall through, fear not, for we have back-ups and fall-backs and stand-ins: in these times, one must prepare for drought, and droughts strike so very slowly such that we find ourselves in the middle of them even though we haven't sensed them coming on, and preparations for drought cannot simply be the setting aside of water; instead, we must set ourselves up for dehydrated life and hence, in the event of furniture provision being less promising than estimated, and if an Orchard cannot grow as previously empty land withers, there is always one more idea, or plan, for the hard times, and this plan derives from the propensity of people to prepare themselves for the worst – sharing your pessimistic persona, I suppose, but without the wit – and after raising a small amount of capital in partnership with existing insurance industry players this new kind of insurance won't simply compensate for loss of income and desiccation of economic opportunity but will translate that loss into sustenance – in the future, cash money may be readily available but, given likely severe shortages of furniture and Orchards, it will be difficult to trade it for anything solid and sustaining – the system of trade and purchase on which we have built our expectations may break down irreparably, so imagine, my dearest sister, that compensation will be supplied not in cash but in water and food, which we will warehouse from the proceeds of premiums, and I'm in the process of making appointments to speak with senior management at several major insurance service providers to offer them this chance, once appropriate non-disclosures are entered into, of course, and of course I would prefer not to do this all on my own, so if this is the plan which is most appealing to you …

You seem a little glazed, translucent carbonates or oxides through which your underlying earthenware skin may be glimpsed. After all, some people are lucky to have a single idea in their entire lives, and here am I sharing plan after plan, each one ready to act upon, to action, as I've heard said in corporate circles. I slice the remaining part of the sandwich into bite-sized pieces, partly for convenience and partly just to allow you a little more time to consider, to choose among the offerings I have laid out, and you have finished your sandwich. You lean back and cross your arms, perhaps too closed-off, perhaps still thoughtful.

Would you like some notepaper? A pencil? Would you like me to run through the Orchard again? I'll be making a few appointments tomorrow or the day after. Perhaps you'd like to come along, but I'd definitely have to let them know ahead of time, given that these are senior executives who can't just have unexpected team-members showing up in their offices without appointments.

I press my finger onto the remaining two or three crumbs and pop them into my mouth. Good sandwiches, I say. Thanks. You're offering to lend me twenty dollars — another twenty dollars, you say — because you're my sister and because these ideas or plans, these plans, might take a little while before they begin to produce significant returns.

Up/Down

1

On the wing of the aircraft, someone has stencilled 'Do not walk outside this area', but I am pacing the trolley-width aisle like a technician who has escalated the call to Level Two and is waiting on hold as the irate client also waits on hold and the fact (or, to be more accurate, *figuration*) that the client has placed the pacing technician *on speaker* signifies therefore that this imaginary technician has been transfigured into – *has become* – a conduit for the script which values your call and will be with you as soon as possible but doesn't cherish your call enough to consider whether or not you may be further irritated by a cover of 'Greensleeves' played by a single robot programmed by no one who attended the Conservatorium of Music.

Below the area designated by 'Do not walk outside this area' are clouds and a distorted blueness.

If you were standing in the permitted area but unluckily deplaned because of the nine hundred kilometres per hour thing, you might spiral in tuck or pike position through the clouds, which would not feel as jagged and ice-laden as they appeared, and drop into that distorted blueness which would fix itself razorly, azurely into focus before de-escalating to the level below.

2

Forty centimetres along the aircraft wing towards the cabin from 'Do not walk outside this area', someone has affixed a yellow clip or widget with two holes. The clip or widget looks like a cartoon frog, tensed to jump. If you wished not to be swept from the wing – you know, because of the nine hundred kilometres per hour thing – you could fasten yourself to the clip or widget with a carabiner or two and crouch there, frog-like, beside the cartoon frog.

Lunchtime

At that time I gambled every day. These were secret times to speak with myself of my allegiance to the blank passing of hours. Every day, every evening, I lost myself. During those first few months when I was still able to retain my job, each lunchtime I found a pub to spend an hour on the poker machines. Later, of course, I had much more time. I feel no shame, looking back, and perhaps I was a different person. Nonetheless, I am told it is empowering to confess.

At the time I generally parked my old brown Holden on Victoria Street, convenient for a fast escape. One particular lunchtime, I had decided to drive to a certain pub in Paddington where the machines paid slightly better for a full house. Unfortunately, I discovered that my car had been parked in by a Mercedes convertible, in the passenger seat of which sat a woman speaking on her car phone – that's what they had in those days, the well-off, Mercedeses with car phones. Great, you know, I thought. Terrific. I reached into my car and honked the horn. A rich-looking fat man – gold-watch display counterbalanced poorman's beergut hanging over his shorts – climbed out of the seat behind her and made his entitled way around the Merc.

He looked me over, face to feet: I was wearing a mostly clean T-shirt, old jeans, no shoes. I approached him anyway. You know, had to.

'Do you think you could move this car a couple of metres so I can get out?'

'Which is your car?'

As if he didn't know. I pointed. He gave it disdain.

'She'll only be ten minutes.' He walked away.

The woman had wound down her window for some reason. On the car phone she said, 'I'm obviously not going to get anything out of him, Michael. I want you to start proceedings immediately.'

On the opposite side of the road a Rolls was double-parked in front of a four-storey terrace house. The fuck with all the double-parking. I mean, really. Another big fat man – this one with a receding hairline and greasy hair pulled back into a ponytail – sat impassively in the driver's seat. Between the two men, a few good strides up Ugly Avenue. And what the fuck is it with sitting in the double-parked cars? What is that? Really. Two slightly shorter than usual blond police stood on the pavement behind the Rolls, guards of bloody honour.

The woman on the phone said, 'I'll just go and get a police officer to talk to you.'

She put the phone down on the passenger seat and crossed the road. I leaned on the roof of my car, twitchy. I could have leaned in and torn the phone from its moorings.

A deodorised cop came and sat in the passenger seat of the Merc, to talk on that car phone. The woman and the man in shorts now stood on the driver's side. Second fat man turned his Rolls-Royce around in the street and parked behind the Mercedes. He got out, approached the woman, said something, walked back towards the Rolls.

The woman said, 'You can't just walk away. I have a right to get my things. You can't just leave.'

She tried to grab him. He pushed her away and got into the Rolls. She followed him, reached in through the driver's window and tried to grab him again. He accelerated and she let go. The Rolls moved around the Mercedes and along Victoria Street. The woman burst into tears, returned to stand beside the Merc. The first fat man put his arms around her.

Other cop crossed the road. The first was still talking on the car phone. He walked around to my side of the Mercedes. I tried again.

'Do you think this car could be moved a couple of metres? I have to get going and I've been stuck here for a long time already, please understand.'

'Where are you going?'

'Up the road.'

'Doesn't sound too urgent to me. Why don't you walk?'

'Too far.'

'Ah well, shouldn't be long.' Turned his back to me.

A tall, slim man carried a cardboard box out of the terrace house towards the Merc.

He said to the woman, 'These are your things from around and on the desk. Everything.'

'Don't say anything,' said her man.

She didn't say anything. The thin man deposited the box on the bitumen beside her, smiled briefly, returned to the house. Everyone else stood around as though they'd run out of choreography.

Sometimes the waiting is endless. The testing goes on and on, fascinating and tiring, and can never replace desire.

ClickBait

Their knees touched beneath an inner table at This Amazingly Protective Cat, one of Eight Local Restaurants You Wouldn't Believe Could Fit Adult-Sized People.

He was saying, 'I really want to let you know my news that will change the way you think about me forever, but first we'll need to have ten minutes of standard informational conversation.'

She pressed her lips together and gave a brief but sufficient nod. It was clear to both of them why when communicating – for all purposes from business to flirting – subtle needn't mean ineffective, and both were aware of Thirteen Unlucky Reasons Blunt Can Be Counterproductive.

He clocked the nod and she read approval in his eyes. They had been seeing each other for two years at a certain level – rare theatre or movie visits, once-weekly restaurant and once- or twice-weekly bed. He felt he was a good lover. He'd already been a practitioner of the best four of Seven Sure-Fire Tips to Make Your Girlfriend Squeal. She had squealed frequently, he noted, though she remained not at all keen on the term 'girlfriend'. There were, after all, at least six better and legal alternatives. He'd accepted her parameters without much enthusiasm, but on the other hand too much choice can literally waste three years of your life. Plus, he was not going to run his love life like a high-school debate by letting semantics take over. He felt in control of 90 per cent, or 80, of his life.

As far as her reasons, he tried to understand these as best he could and he accepted that the future could not yet be read. Hesitancy and reluctance were neither a pair of hibernating bears nor twinned deciduous trees: there was nothing that would inevitably awaken or sprout. And yet there was between them a certain equilibrium: not one of Three Definitive Signs Your Relationship Is Terminal had arrived.

This evening, she was slightly distracted and her glance seemed to him drawn towards her hands, which were under the table, or her thighs – though this instinctual impression was, he knew, a Hard-to-Lose Twentieth-Century Habit, and the truth was certainly that her pubic area was well covered by two layers of clothing and her phone's true high-definition screen.

'It's funny you should say that,' she said, her look benign-neutral rather than amused. 'According to 62 per cent of communications specialists, meta-conversation is on the way out.'

Her right hand slipped from the table and she watched it descend, but she pulled her gaze back to him before its fingers could recommence their pecking.

'I wonder if it's the same 62 per cent who claimed psychology had died. You remember? Once everybody understood how their unconscious signals would be interpreted, they gestured powerfully and competently, with an eye to advancement. Anyway, sounds like we're among the recalcitrant 38 who continue to talk the talk.'

'Mm, we must be slow learners, despite the shocking new evidence that we've changed the way we speak *without even noticing*. Anyway, it couldn't be the same 62 per cent because under 1 per cent of them would have known Two Simple Investment Rules to Retire Luxuriously Early but a larger and unfortunate subset had never encountered Four Surprising Factors Which Lengthen Your Life by Decades.'

'Bahamas or Death.'

'Exactly.'

The waitress's natural thinness allowed her somehow to arrive beside their table. They had decided to age beautifully and naturally, so forwent the recommended green and red juices and selected a Souzao for him and a Roussanne/ Picpoul for her from the wine list of Five Unmissable Varietals You Never Heard Of.

'I'll come back for your food order,' the waitress said.

'Sure, thank you.'

Every successful salesperson knows how much a single glass of wine increases impulsivity, but they didn't.

His blue shirt nonetheless reflected the momentary blue light near its junction with the table. There was another opportunity which would only last ten minutes or until sold, but he put the phone back in his pocket.

'Here's something weird,' he began. 'Yesterday, I was on a bus which passed through three of the Next Four Boom Suburbs, when I was momentarily overcome by the feeling ...'

'Oh. My. God,' she said. 'Look at that.'

Her eyes gestured above and to her right, where the actor Geena Davis had entered.

'See how confident she looks at fifty-seven,' she said – the actor had lived through an apprehensive childhood because of her height, and she was not much shorter now.

'She's also incredibly smart,' he said. 'Like, Ten Smartest Actresses smart.'

'It's funny how many public figures you wouldn't expect to find in Mensa,' she agreed.

'Shall I continue?' he asked, careful not to tinge his voice with intonations that alienate.

'Ah yes, ordinary bus rides through extraordinary sights.' She was a little edgy, in the old sense, but seemed to make an effort to focus.

'I thought I would see fireworks. I felt I had been there before, that we would turn a corner to the left and there would be, exactly that, extraordinary sights.'

'Yeah. Those moments when you experience phenomena scientists will never disprove.'

'Kind of. Because they will disprove it but we won't believe them. And around the corner, there was a burning building, four or five storeys high. I got off the bus. I can't actually remember getting up from my seat, or anything until I was standing in the street – the bus must have stopped because the road was obviously obstructed – and I walked even closer. People were still running out the front door and fire alarms were going off. There was a woman waving and screaming something out of the third-floor window. It was incredibly noisy. People were yelling at her to jump. Everyone was shouting even though no one could hear anything.

She stepped back from the window and disappeared for a moment, but then we saw her again. Someone had a blanket, and everyone was holding it stretched out, like firemen in the movies, and I was also holding an edge of the blanket, not knowing whether it would be strong enough, or what it would feel like if we caught her. The woman started throwing flowers down on us and, oddly, there we were catching these white and yellow flowers in the blanket and screaming to her to jump. We could feel the intensity of the heat and at that moment a fire truck arrived, one of the firemen went straight up a ladder and grabbed her, she didn't resist. I could see the whole thing but was backing off, or we were being pushed back by police, and she came down the ladder with this fireman and was throwing flowers the whole time, don't know how she held so many, and when she got to the bottom she was still shouting, and I heard what she was saying, which was, "My garden! My garden!"'

'Wow.' She had teared up a little, one escaped down her face, and she made no effort to disguise it. Revealing emotions is a sign of strength, anyway.

'It was like a series of You Won't Believe What Happens Next. It was amazing, and there was no way to share it because everyone was acting impulsively.'

'But you just shared it,' she said.

'You know what I mean.'

'Yes. Kind of stream-of-consciousness.'

Geena Davis was eating pancakes, and her companion taking notes – a journalist, most likely.

Near Miss

A crash, an echo, the steady background drone of insects with punctuating, arrhythmic birds carrying some harsh melody.

He had not recovered from the drive. His ears still hummed with the sounds of the road – well, that was normal – but moreover he was still shaky and still actually shaking from the near miss, the swerve away from the looming vehicle with that glimpse of the old man's terrified stare caught in the sunlight. In the rear-view mirror he had seen the trailer swing out into the road behind him and back again, a sick metronome proffering the chance of death, though no one had died. He saw in the rear-view the other car pull across to the side. The old man must have been shaking too.

He thought for a moment to stop, turn around, check on the old man's condition, but he was a little angry, or very angry, hard to tell. What could he have said? Are you recovering from putting me at risk? Can I suggest you stay seated and do not restart the car. Why were such drivers still permitted? It was best that he had not stopped. The confrontation could be played out in his mind without having to subject a living human to his Gestalt moment.

He had driven a little further but pulled over at the point marked Rest Area and stared for a long time through the windscreen, through a barbed wire fence, at the intense green field in that late afternoon light. He wasn't even thinking about luck. He took a couple of gulps from his water bottle and thought it tasted delicious. Afterwards, he was conscious of slowing his car, staying a few kilometres per hour below the speed limit. Another hour – it would usually have taken him thirty-five minutes – and he took the old gravel road off to the left, just past the lumberyard. As it wound its way through the hills he opened his window to admit the scent of the eucalyptus forest: faintly minty, he thought, but really the finer points of scent were beyond his capability. The blunt aspects, that all the air that had been in the car when the old man almost killed him had now been replaced by new, non-killer atmosphere, this he comprehended. And he drove more slowly along here than he ever had before.

Tomorrow, Niamh would arrive and the near miss would have faded from his consciousness. He tried to think of Niamh now, tried to conjure up her scent, but his mind kept pulling him back to that moment, the swerve, glimpse of the trailer swinging out in his rear-view.

He was moving again now, drawing out of the Rest Area, but so slowly that perhaps he could have run faster. Tomorrow, the image might lose its insistence. Driving was, in some ways, a constant spate of near misses, all the roads tightly packed and everyone losing concentration with great frequency. No one could possibly remember them all, the feints into wrong lanes, brakes applied just in time, vehicles hurtling through yellow-turning-red traffic lights, pulling out to see around impossibly parked trucks only to find other trucks advancing at speed. It was a wonder there were so few accidents, perhaps some evolutionary watchman trait, a quirk whereby in the species only a small proportion lost concentration at any one time, leaving all the others to look out for them or to stay out of their way. Is this something Niamh would have said? She would have found words of comfort from somewhere, most likely. Niamh was good in a crisis. He tried to replace the flashbacks with images of her, or to insert Niamh into every scenario: there she was, driving a little yellow car, stopping after an accident to offer assistance. She was the police officer. Ha! The thought of her uniformed was ludicrous enough to break in.

Even at this speed, he was making progress. He passed the doll mansion, as he and Niamh had named it, a dwelling comprising a rectangle of old planks and corrugated iron with pink stripes painted here and there, flywire instead of glass for windows, though compensated for by a couple of skilfully rendered *trompe l'oeil* windows and a pair of less artful Doric columns either side of a crappy old door, or an antiqued mock-original entrance boasting (as a real estate agent might put it) an arch of plastic dolls. The doll mansion marked one kilometre to go, and shortly after he pulled up beside his own little shack, climbed from the car and sat heavily on the ground. He was surprised by how weak he felt, needing some sweet tea perhaps. The shack itself was a bit more than the name suggested: three rooms, a generous and well-made veranda around three sides, running water. There was even mostly reliable electricity and a couple of years earlier he'd brought up a good mattress.

Heaving himself back to his feet, he pulled a couple of bags of food out of the car boot, carried them into the kitchen, leaving them on the floor. Inside the shack, it was chilly, so no urgency to refrigerate anything. He switched the fridge on and removed the wedge, which was supposed to prevent mustiness.

Back outside, he made his way to the top of the slope in the southern corner of the yard and sat on a log to catch the last of the afternoon sun, its heat on his face amidst the chill of the forest rising with the mist from the valley floor. Orange beefsteak fungus grew in clumps around the base of a blackened stump. The moss at his feet had gone to seed. Further away in the forest there was a creaking sound, a cricket or if he was lucky it might have been a gang-gang cockatoo and he might catch sight of it. When Niamh arrived they could take the path, which followed an old watercourse into the valley, from the southern side of the property. The southern side of his *estate*, as she insisted. He hoped his hearing would have recovered fully by then; he felt a little muddy inside, not pleasant, and although it wasn't the kind of discomfort he would mention to Niamh, he hated feeling that he was holding back – better to have nothing to complain about in the first place.

In the distance a dog yapped, a day early for it to have been warning of Niamh's arrival. He had a sudden image of her at twenty, striking and confident, as they'd leaned against the sun-warmed cement university wall. That instant. He had been so taken with her, gripped. He remembered the moment of thinking, there in the patch of sunlight: aah, so this is love. How could two people kiss so slowly? The feeling of her through all those winter layers of clothing and *sumer*, as it was said, *is icumen in.*

As if, he thought to himself, as if he hadn't stayed in love with her, that feeling – however it happened – that was beyond attraction. They had all been so beautiful, he knew in retrospect, the blanket of beauty that was youth, but she was still as beautiful. Yes, that look she had, oh my God, differently beautiful now apart from that look, that's true, and she was less harsh in her judgement and her expressions of it. As was he. But still, he wondered if they would contest everything this visit as they had on the last, arguing as vehemently about the issues on which they agreed, one or the other trying to find distinguishments between their mutual adoration of a certain movie or nuanced distinctions in their contempt for some political statement or other. Would he feel obliged to make declarations? Oh Niamh, as if he hadn't said how he felt and, intermittently, rarely coinciding, she had.

A blowfly roared by like a motorcycle, that's how he phrased it to himself, the thing veering around the mountain roads of the air, a motorcycle *through the blind spot*, and he was back to recalling the image of the fear in the old driver's eyes. Dammit, there it was again. He tried to let the picture go, or to force it out of his mind by turning the views to instrumental purpose, watching the coils of mist moving across the valley. Cicadas picked up their chanting all at once, last chorus of the day, in response to some shift he couldn't pick out. That last slice of crimson sun dipped another degree behind the forested ridge to the north-west and was gone from his yard. He pulled the jacket tighter. Around him, the Australian bush took on its twilit duotone, greys for the earth and sky, shades of orange at the horizon. He walked across to the undamaged car, pulled his bag from the back seat, and one last box of fruit. He would put the shack in order, creating an impression of himself as newly organised, latterly matured. Imagine what she would make of that misrepresentation.

The little house cooled substantially at night and he stacked his usual meticulous fire, struck the match against strips of dry newspaper, which took immediately. Here he was, mesmerised again, willing the heat to fill the little room, shifting the twigs a little, leaning in to direct his breath at the fire's base, having faith that choosing the correct angle would cause the fire to strengthen as always, conscious of faith despite the fire always taking, so skilled he was. And there it went, flames searching for a grip around the heavy log he'd laid on top. These were the moments when he didn't mind the solitude and for a moment he almost regretted having asked Niamh to join him and especially the self-weakening way he'd asked her so that they both felt the weight of the anticipation. He threw a few small sticks in; the fire had caught well and there was no purpose other than to watch them burn away, olive-tinted leaves catching in an instant, leaving an outline of glowing points before falling away into ashes. How would it be this time tomorrow, building the fire but with no monopoly on it, he and Niamh taking it in turns to play with it or duelling for the right to turn a branch? Would she kiss him? Should he kiss her? What if, after all this time, the attraction felt only nostalgic, the desire a memory of the desire he'd once experienced? He had no answers to these. What if he took one look at her and felt everything all again? That was a better question to contemplate.

He dragged his bedding down beside the fire and lay on his side, staring into the pulsing coals. After a while he slept.

Niamh floored it around the semitrailer, pulled back in. The car shook, this noisy old bastard. Here she went again, Andre and his hilarious Folly, the Estate. He was the most sentimental human she had ever fallen in love with, and slow-moving too. Such arms in which to enfold, his bear hug and his repartee, one then the other. The wine bottles clicked together behind her seat. She intended to stay there for some time. I'll be out of contact till I'm back in, she had written, and I'm fine so relax. At twenty-five he'd decided on the bush block – all decisions made at twenty-five are the correct ones, he'd said. How right he'd been, though neither of them really knew it. We should live together up there, he'd said. What about life, she'd replied. Bring it, he'd said. A mere two decades later, they were still mid-conversation, and just now she was thinking maybe, maybe.

She took the turn-off, wound her way along the unmade road, passed the doll mansion. There he was as she pulled up, standing out the front of his Folly, grinning like a fool. She shoved open the car door, already laughing, and he started laughing too, and he strode forward to pull her out of there and inside.

PART II

PART II

Lingua Franca

Sin titulación
My mother got whacked in the ear with a small fish and now she's hard of herring. Translate that into French, M. Blanchaille.

She folded the piece into a small envelope, wrote his address on the front, no return address, stuck a stamp on, wandered around the corner to the postbox.

Ella fue horneada
She received a postcard with a URL scrawled across it in green ink, barely legible – strangely, the obverse depicted a birthday cake. She typed the address into her browser. A message on the screen flashed greenly on and off at her: *Don't go to too much blinking trouble, Señora Pestaña.*

Fucsia profondo
Across town, he received a pot plant from a floral delivery firm. The pot was plain – terracotta – and the plant was a maidenhair fern with a nursery label tied to it with dark pink cotton. The label read: *There are enough bald statements in the world already, Herr Herausfallen.*

She laughed from time to time, thinking of his German-illiterate face, enlarged by hairline recession.

Un sexto de vida
Once again with the aging process, he thought, the one thing I cannot mitigate. They had known each other a long time. He sighed. He clicked. Niente. The internet was on the blink and on the nose. He had to repost his riposte. *The longer it goes, the longer it grows, the less she knows. Non è così, Signora Setto?*

No se arrugarse
Señor Pliegue, who bothers whom? read the newly sprayed red graffito running along the corridor outside his office. And it continued, smaller, in black marker pen: *Shall we not meet near the butcher's or the bookshop? I'll be one turn ahead.*

She was
allí.

Further Notes to the
Monkey Problem

After the title, Hamlet, *and preceding a faultlessly typed manuscript of that play, a monkey had typed a clear, concise foreword explaining productive methodology.*

We have often heard Ferdinand de Saussure lament the dearth of principles and methods that marked linguistics during his developmental period. Partly in tribute to him and partly as a salute to Professore Vetano, the pioneer of this program, I offer this foreword to my current translation of Shakespeare's *Hamlet*.

As so many have argued, and eloquently, 'Writing is not something that can be taught.' We have discovered that it is an entirely random activity, its randomness checked only by the calligraphic limitations of the keyboard. Nevertheless, a certain intentionality may be imputed in that, within those parameters, no monkey's practice was otherwise delimited by teaching or other discipline. It follows, then, that what we were undertaking was indeed 'writing' and this 'writing' was of an exceedingly pure species. We were untaught as James Joyce himself was untaught. He had only the tools of the craft before him, produced without the premonition of greatness. Joyce had greatness thrust upon him in what became his epoch. This has become known as our epoch, the epoch of the Monkey House.

Six months ago, Vetano told me I was lucky. I do not deny it. I am lucky to work in such an environment; I am lucky my patrons are so supportive of myself and my colleagues; I am lucky that, of all the monkeys in the Monkey House, I was the one to produce *Hamlet*; and I am lucky Vetano's research assistant, Mr Juredovich, discovered my work and published it for all the world to share and enjoy. I am lucky, but if I were not, another monkey might have received the glory or, perhaps, the work would never have been written. This discussion holds no interest for me. I have done what I have done and, if I have done it without pride, then I am modest or else incapable of pride, unlearned in folly.

One of the major criticisms directed against our practice is that it is not 'artistic'. Now, while I do not hold that 'any monkey can be an artist' (Bonzo, 'k;vbip' [unpublished manuscript], c. 1923, p. 18,622), I would argue most strongly that our practice is an artistic one. What chance is there, for instance, that this work will be discovered within my lifetime? Many great works produced within the Monkey House have been consigned by their authors to the garbage heap, lost to history and to eternity. Many great authors have died, undiscovered and never to be discovered. This is what 'art' is, a breath of air in a *gewitter* of activity. Our workshop environment is that thunderstorm, the rates of production incredible. And we work hard, always seeking that gust of genius, that Truth, that fleeting chain of characters which overflows with meaning.

Now to the production of *Hamlet*. Critics have asked, as critics will, what a monkey would know of Denmark. I have seen Vetano respond angrily, shouting, 'Have you read this work? Have you?' I have only sympathy with the Professore's position but shall here attempt a fuller reply. If a critic were to ask me what I know of Denmark, unless that critic were a monkey, I probably would not understand. If I were to understand, the critic (unless a monkey) would not understand my reply. Now suppose the critic did understand my reply and I spoke not about Denmark, but about something quite different. A responsive critic would search for connection, for *metafora*, for the meaning in my response. Yet this is not the criticism I have received. And why? Because intelligence is not imputed to me. If I should type not of Denmark, does that mean I know not of Denmark? It does not. I know of the arms of my love yet type not of them. Or perhaps I know not of them. Either way there need be no relation between experience and product. I do not pretend to write autobiography. I am not the King of Denmark, nor am I an historian of the Danish Royal Court. All I ask is that this work be considered as it stands for you, the reader or performer. I did not think on you when I wrote; now you must not think on me.

Lastly, ten thousand monkeys took part in Vetano's literary program. Their participation provided me with the support, the incentive to continue. As I saw them rewarded for their efforts, so did I redouble mine. I learned much from them, and I am privileged to believe that some of them have learned from me. It is to these monkeys, my colleagues, that I dedicate *Hamlet*.

Fifty Responses to the
Ravens Paradox*

'I am a raven,' said the white shoe.

'I imagine you are,' said someone at the end of the great extinction.

'Is this one-legged bird a raven?' asked the blind woman.

'It tends to be,' answered a man with a one-armed brother.

'No, because I have painted it green or blue,' said the artist.

'Intrinsically,' said the white shoe.

'What's that behind your back?' Magellan asked you know who. 'I have travelled the world and have seen every living raven *but one*, and I'm hoping to complete my survey.'

'I'm also interested,' said Elcano. 'I believe I have seen every raven, and have looked everywhere except behind your back and behind her back, but I might have missed one or possibly two.'

'Behind my back is a box which may or may not contain something black,' said you know who.

---

* This is a story about inductive reasoning. Or a non-story (see inside). It's about requirements for confirming or disconfirming the hypothesis 'All ravens are black'.

'We want to see it,' chorused the travellers.

'I also have a box,' she (unidentified) said. 'This box contains a red raven, but I'm not sure if it's alive.'

'I don't believe you,' said the white shoe.

'If it's red, it can't be a raven,' said a man of faith.

'I am a raven,' said a crow. 'Pretty much a raven, anyway. Do you believe me?'

'Yes. I'm very open-minded,' said the white shoe, 'in a particular fashion.'

'I have to check your DNA,' said the absolutist, whose name I've forgotten but whose type has stuck in my mind.

'Well, I feel like I'm a raven,' said the crow.

'I'll check your DNA,' repeated the absolutist. 'I'll check it twice to make sure.'

'What colour is my DNA?' asked the crow, and took off, very fast.

'A raven is flying towards me at close to the speed of light, as I fly towards it at close to the speed of light,' remarked a photon.

'I polished my feathers to make them more reflective,' said the flying crow, breathlessly.

'I see what you mean,' said the (possibly) lateral tree in a forest.

'Obviously I can't see that,' said the utterly static absolutist.

'Cute, but small,' commented someone. 'In this infinite universe, there are bound to be uncountable planets occupied by ravens. Not all ravens can be observed.'

'So we're not just projecting ravens, we have to project planets?' said no one.

'There are languages which cannot conceive of ravens,' said Artemis.

'Then they are not languages,' said Harry the hegemonist.

'The darkness is coming,' said a man at Speakers' Corner, 'rhetorically.'

'I see all,' said someone omniscient, 'but I can only speak in analogies.'

'Will you tell us at the end of time?' beseeched many, many people.

'You're spinning me out,' said someone really stoned at a music festival. 'Ravens are like super smart, so they'd tell us straightaway if only we could learn to listen. I mean, have you seriously checked out a raven's neural pathways?'

'Formulate this, punk,' said a multidisciplinary research team. 'You're the one who's a mess.'

'I've nearly found a recessive gene for colour,' said the white shoe. 'Do you believe me now?'

'No,' said a nihilist, 'and you know why.'

'I don't think this is a story, but I like it,' said Pola the real person.

'If not a story, what is it?' I (the real I) asked.

'If I hold it behind my back, it could be a raven,' said real Pola in the real world, but not really 'said' unless the category 'said' includes messages mediated through mobile telephony.

'This qualification may also apply to "asked" and "observed",' noted an imaginary friend, who is maybe a raven.

'I am not a raven,' said the almost certainly black raven or black non-raven or non-black non-raven held out of sight behind someone's fictional back. 'I've been read my rights so you can use this statement as evidence in a court of law.'

'That's worthless information,' said a judicial officer, 'or infinitesimally useful, which in practical terms means the same thing.'

'I'm practically a raven,' said the crow.

'Me too,' said the white shoe, 'and I have a character arc about identity.'

'I am and I am not, plus I'm not practical at all,' said a voice from inside a box.

'I'm pretty sure the small details contribute,' echoed Archimedes of Syracuse through history. 'Also, in this story we follow the ravens from a relatively small and fully accountable population through to an incalculable number in an infinite and infinitely marvellous and enigmatic universe of corvid uniformity or diversity.'

'Stop perorating,' said a Pola (not the real one). 'It's not a story.'

A raven appeared out of nowhere. No one could determine its hue.

'I get the last word,' said the white shoe.

Everyone agreed.

The New Class Is Troubling

The curricular vector and the vector of learning are two skew lines through a non-ideal vacuum. This new class is troubling, worse than the previous one, and I wish I hadn't asked to be moved. In retrospect, the haste with which my request was acceded to was regrettably portentous and I should have foreseen that no good would come of the change. The principal, Flederman, in agreeing to the shift, seemed overly pleased. He shook my hand, wished me luck for the only time.

From that office, I made my way along the corridors to the most isolated end of the school, imagining – though surely this was impossible – that I continued to feel the press of Principal Flederman's hand on mine. My new classroom was audible some tens of metres before it became visible. Its volume in no way diminished as I entered, nor did any student acknowledge by greeting or otherwise that I had entered. I headed towards the front. At first glance, the room seemed to contain chairs and tables in the correct allocation, but the spread of furniture did not intersect in any manner with clustered student orbits.

'Ahem. Good morning,' I said, writing my name up on

the board. I repeated, somewhat louder, 'Good morning! My name is Semmet. I'll be your teacher from now. Please take your seats.'

'Hello, Semmet,' called out three or four of them.

'We can't sit down,' said someone else. 'We haven't all had a turn yet.'

It was not at all clear what their referent was.

'You'll have to do it later,' I said.

Someone laughed.

'What's funny?' I asked, straining to avoid tonal sharpness.

There may have been some further effort to suppress laughter, and the students began to shuffle towards desks. Instead of sitting though, they continued to move around, as if unsure of which desk belonged to whom. There seemed some kind of parcel they were passing this way and that, an Ella handing it off to a Marcus (this is not definitive as I didn't yet know their names), the Marcus smuggling it into the hands of a Charlie and so forth. The uncertainty of their movements crystallised into a kind of choreography, all based upon passing the object and disguising it from me.

'Right,' I said, hanging on to my temper as best as I could. 'Let's see that.'

The choreography led ten or twelve students towards the door, which opened and shut immediately. The students finally began sitting. I opened the door, peered around to the left and right, but saw nothing. I heard someone laugh behind me, but when I turned around, no one was laughing and no one was looking at me.

'Right,' I said again. 'The roll. Andrea?'

No answer.

'Andrea? Is she here?'

'She's called Ella now,' said a voice.

'Is that true?'

'Yes,' said several voices.

'Okay then. Where is the Ella who used to be Andrea?'

'Here, sir.'

Someone snickered.

'Anita.'

'Here, sir,' said the same girl.

I looked at her as sternly as I could.

'I'm on the list twice,' she said. 'It's always been like that.'

As it began, so it went on.

And on.

Portents of ill continued to manifest, or to metamorphose from portents into full-grown ill. Aspects of the new class were not as they should have been. There was, it seemed to me, a sense of unnaturalness in the room. The boy called Harry looked like he should be an Oliver. Equally, the Oliver was suggestive of a Harry. I tried to call them by their true names – and at times did so inadvertently – but both acted somehow offended and protested with much more vociferousness than a mere name-switch ought to have precipitated. Too much protest? I could not guess at what drove their fervour.

The several girls called Ella formed a diagonal across the room, back left to front right, whether by chance or habit or intent. They had little in common. I was not yet sure which of them had been misnamed. Perhaps all? At the time I continued to call them each by the name Ella and extracted a low rate of response.

There were three Marcuses. One was fourteen, one thirteen and the third claimed to be sixteen though was noted down as twelve. There may have been some sort of rule or prior arrangement which prevented all Marcuses from looking simultaneously in the same direction.

Of the eleven Sams, Charlies and Georges, six were female, three male and two had left the gender box blank. In my previous class, no child left the gender box blank. No questions were raised. This was not a complaint, as one might say to Principal Flederman, who would in my experience misconstrue, but simply a recognition: classroom administration was from the old and classroom inhabitants were from the new. With regard to this grouping, the overarching complaint was and had been and is the same as for all their classmates: the pupils seemed not to recognise the structure within which they were placed. I pointed this out to them but they seemed not to hear. Complaint attracted the same degree of rectification from the entirety of the class as any of my criticisms of and advice to them: precisely none.

Although my role in the new class was, I supposed, as it had been in my former class – to convey to these students information and techniques previously unknown to them and to revise those that they knew – there was almost no correspondence between role and actual function. For example, a large proportion of my function turned out to be identifying and confronting trouble. There was trouble in that room and my job was to face it.

117

The children were not supposed to face trouble at all. They were supposed to face me. Not so many of them practised the facing. Instead, they configured themselves into five exclusive and exclusivist conclaves or enclaves. Occasionally a spokesperson for one of the enclaves or conclaves addressed me with demands or borderline threats, especially if I had attempted to draw attention to the trouble and/or the extent to which the children were facing it rather than me. For example, one of them might say, please would I moderate my tone, or perhaps stop speaking. The tone I was using might upset someone and that would be a pity. Also the words.

I explained that my role was not to placate, mollify and assuage. The spokespeople were direct on this one: I was, they said, wrong. What about my feelings? I said. How about mollifying me? Subdued laughter.

Unfortunately, I lacked reference points for almost all aspects of the non-curricular learning. This, also unfortunately, stemmed from a fortnight of enforced ostracism from my colleagues and supervisors due to what Principal Flederman perceived as my non-collegial tendencies.

At that initial meeting in which Principal Flederman allocated the class to me, I had politely enquired as to whether this would be a permanent shift or whether there would be some form of trial period. Deputy Principal Glass had quipped that the only trial period was a trial-by-ordeal, whereupon Principal Flederman had laughed and counselled me not to worry. When I protested that this very admonition might induce the opposite in me, he laughed a second time and claimed that the children were really very good *deep down*.

'That's even worse,' I said, though perhaps with a tinge of lightness in my tone.

'Are you a complainer?' Principal Flederman had said, demeanour switched in an instant. 'I don't like complainers. Had I known you were one, if you had responded truthfully to the question in the interview about complaining, you might not have been appointed. You'd best keep that in mind. Please come and speak to me in two weeks when the effects of your complaint have worn off.'

'But,' I said.

The flat-smiling Deputy Glass guided me out the door and that was that.

Consequently, given the seeming overthrow of the expected order, I had no local or contemporaneous framework for principles of classroom governance.

Instead, I slowly accumulated questions and unexplained observations. I noted these down day by day, and read over them each afternoon in the quiet of the empty corridors after class ended. There were so many issues to discuss. Who would have thought the new class could provoke so much contemplation? When the trial fortnight finished, and I would be once more permitted to address Principal Flederman, I was hoping to have prioritised my questions, but these seemed not to bend to priorities, remaining somewhat scattered and hard to categorise.

As mentioned there was the question of the Marcuses' sightlines. Further, did the dry-skinned Ella who wished the windows opened take precedence over the Charlie with hayfever who wished the windows shut and the air conditioner running on maximum? If a chair broke, was there some order in which children should be deprived of seating, or was this at the teacher's discretion? Regarding the children who were thus displaced, should addressing this lack fall to the classroom teacher, or was it more a question for administrators?

On the subject of learning, should testing relate to that which had been covered (including extracurricular elements such as classroom architecture, choreography and rhetoric of complaint) or must only the documented curriculum be examined? If the latter, can hints be given (whether or not under the duress of isolation) or a secret pattern incorporated into the multiple choice sections such that further skills in guessing and intimation might also receive rewards?

It occurred to me that the best solution for the gender box issue would be to remove it altogether. This might seem an overreaction given that there were only two non-indicators in the entire room, but I could think of no reason to continue to collect this data. The children themselves were completely indifferent to it, and became restive whenever I attempted to discuss it, whether or not the discussion was aimed at completing the classification of the remaining Sams, Charlies and Georges. If additional data were required, for example if our circumstance required that a set amount of data be retained, perhaps a box on preferred hours would have been more valuable, so as to identify the afternoon children who ought to be under less pressure in the mornings, and the morning children who were at their best first thing. Could I put forward this suggestion without raising further ire and risking Principal Flederman imposing a further period of verbal exile?

I tried to discuss the competing demands with representatives from each of the conclaves or enclaves. I tried to convene meetings in which the contents of tests were communicated to the various groups. This was not successful. Instead, several of the groups refused to put forward representatives for this purpose, or stipulated that representatives would only be put forward for alternative agendas wherein any mention of tests or testing was impermissible. When I nominated a representative for a non-compliant group, the representative either refused to come forward or was rejected by the group on their attempt to return bearing the information from our meeting. Three children were ostracised as a result, following which those three agreed to share a further table. At their new table, they continued to purport to represent their conclaves or enclaves but their rulings and suggestions were not listened to. Further, they bickered at volume about which of the three ought to represent the table at which they now sat.

My own testing two weeks of isolation approached its end. I noted the eleven days passed, and three still to go, by means of an accumulation of exes on a calendar near my desk – although this record may not have been reliable as several additional marks had been appended by person or persons unknown. If I lasted this time out – no, I told myself, I would last these final days so as to put these many important questions to Principal Flederman.

In the generic fantasy, after struggling for a few months, or maybe fourteen days, the teacher makes the kind of rousing speech in which he, she or I convince an apparent rabble, this apparent rabble, that each is an individual with the power to change her or his or their own lives. In return, they (all except one hold-out) transcend the institutional structures which, though supposedly set up to support struggling or recalcitrant students, in fact exclude them, and with their new clear vision (all except one hold-out) they understand their own and also my humanity.

The subject matter in this mythic lesson should be a stand-in for the art form to hand, but in this imaginary case it is mathematics. How big would a tennis court on the moon have to be?

It just so happens that my one hold-out loves tennis. Click. I open my eyes.

Day Fourteen, Part I.

I knocked on Deputy Principal Glass's door.

'This new class, either we've got off to a bad start or we're continuing badly.'

'That sounds right,' said Glass.

'Some refuse to sit at desks.'

'So let them stand,' said the deputy. 'What difference could it make?'

'When standing, they seem to listen less.'

'That's not possible.'

'What do you advise?'

'Carry on as you are. Or don't.'

'Thank you,' I said, as expressionlessly as possible.

'I'm sure you'll find your own way through.'

'Sure.' I allowed a small amount of warmth into my voice.

'Or not.'

Perhaps I had been smiling. I felt the expression sag down my face.

Day Fourteen, Part II.

I knocked also on Principal Flederman's door.

'Come.' For some, it is important to save on prepositions. I entered. 'Ah, Semmet. There you are. I hear all is going well.'

'Oh good,' I said, curricular articulation evaporating.

'Delighted to hear it. That class has been a tricky one, at times. But they're good kids, deep down.'

'Yes. I guess they are.'

Given my designation as Teacher, I had been surprised to observe the extent of my own learning. To summarise, it comprised the element of increased acceptance and the element of inversion of expectation, the element of decentred architecture and the element of tolerance, the element of dynamic social reformation and the element of isolation. The children's learning comprised negotiation, blanketing and rhythmic chanting. None of this was noted in the curriculum documents or annexes.

I began to prepare the test papers.

Waltzing Matilda

Brown-bound menus offer the usual egg and chips, sausage and chips, steak and chips choices.

One of four uniformed police at the next table stands up and begins to sing operatically.

'We don't need the fucking requiem,' shouts his colleague. 'Just get on with what you're saying.'

'Amen,' says another.

'Amen to you too, you unappreciative buggers. I was merely trying to illustrate a sense of the solemnity of his crime and to prefigure his tragic end. But if your foreshortened attention spans will only bear the abridged version, that's what I'll give you,' says the singer. 'Okay then, there's wool and blood all over the fucking camp. His trousers are red from the thighs down. He's red-handed too, you could say. And his rucksack's practically still trembling with the poor creature's *rigor mortis*. The grazier's tut-tutting from his horse. Robbie and Tom – know them? – are no doubt gearing up to give him a bit of a hiding on the way back to the station, and I'm the one who sticks to the rigmarole.'

'Constable fucking Procedure,' mutters the shouter.

'You got me right. So I tell him, "We're going to arrest you for the sheep, you silly coot." He stands up and he's looking like he's going to come quietly. I'm thinking, there's a first time for bloody everything. Nice and easy, hands forward ready for the cuffs. World needs more criminals like that, if you ask me, head bowed, fully cognisant of the crime and his likely incarceration.'

'Dead set, mate,' says the amen-er. 'Next thing you'll be inviting him to the Christmas barbecue.'

'A feller like that, and he admitted anything at all,' agrees the first opera-hater. 'Miracles in our lifetime.'

'Ha! Not fucking likely. No cooperation actually happened. Instead he says, "Okay then, haul me in from here, bloody coppers," and he jumps into the bog. No help from us, I swear, much trouble as that stupid bugger has been over the years.'

The fourth begins to laugh. 'That what you told the coroner, is it?'

'What do *you* think, John? "Yes, Your Worship, whilst we had no part in the unfortunate man's actions, and had indeed taken all care to prevent self-harm on his part, we had previously consulted on optimum launch angles and velocities." Wouldn't have minded too much, but of course I wouldn't do it. All my friends'd agree to that about me. In fact, many have in earlier circumstances. Besides, as you know from your own extensive training, such courses of action are against the rules. I don't have a rule-breaking bone in my body.'

'The gentleman doth protest too much, methinks,' says John to the other two, who laugh briefly.

'Well,' admits the storyteller, 'we might not have stood by in entire and unreserved idleness.'

More laughter.

'And the stains on his trousers did require immediate rinsing. But let's agree he pretty much propelled himself. Say 70 per cent self-propulsion. Or at least 60. Anyway, I genuinely liked him, despite his deep-seated recidivist criminality.'

'Yeah right,' says John.

'John, I was a broken man afterwards. I wept for weeks. I loved him like a brother. You ask anyone. Ask his bloody mother.'

'Right,' says John, smirking. 'I might do that.'

'Sure you will. Dig her up and ask her. And while you're spading away, I'll visit that other accident-prone feller's widow out by the dam, see how well she remembers you. Very nice that one, in all her mourning.'

John adds a syllable to his previous utterance: 'Right-o,' and continues, 'Got me there.'

'Thought I did. But listen to this: the old bugger's hardly in the swim for one second and he straight up disappears. Never refloated. No bubbles, not a single fart.'

'Aw,' says one of the others. 'That's very sad.'

'Crying shame, isn't it?' continues the first policeman. 'Grazier, name of Marston, Mr Marston to you, turns around and trots off without a word. Remaining three of us, grade-A coppers all, staring like frillnecks at the flat brown surface. Nothing there, and Tom's panicking straightaway. He's shaking like a baby and he says, "Jeez fellers, what'll we do about this?" Then Robbie – you blokes know him?'

John assents, but the others shake their heads.

'Big, slow fellow, but smart and about as level-headed as a school boater, decides, "No *corpus delicti*. Looks to me a lot like nothing's happened here." He says, "Hang on," and puts his ear near the ground. "Nope. Nothing. No cavalry." Tom gets excited about this method, squeaks out, "No *corpus*, no forms!" and Robbie says, "Amen. *Requiescat in pace*," and I'm saying, "Anyhow, *homo ovi* fucking *lupus*." Three of us never breathed a word to anyone and no one ever asked. Probably no one missed him.'

'Straight in, no splash?' asks the fourth.

'Straight in. What a fucking hero. Makes me want to weep.'

John interjects, 'Weeping's orright. Just don't fucking start singing again. Nellie bloody Melba.'

All laugh.

Fire in My Brain,
That You'd Like to Put Out

The advertising screen at the front of the bus is on silent.
Image after image of laughing consumers, but nothing
to be heard above the engine. Every sequence transforms
a purchaser into an owner, all without adding a decibel.
How can it be 'on silent'? I ask my neighbour. *Why not just
'silent'? Why not 'on silently'?* No comment. I judge that my
neighbour does not wish to participate in this conversation.
If you can spend it, why not? mouths an owner of things on
the screen.

Along the way, we pass mostly temporary buildings.
They have, though, permanent fences.

I photocopy buildings in my head – almost every one
is full-sized. This is something to be proud of, though I
have been asked not to speak of it. Some of the fences are
also fitted with swinging gates. I could take the buildings
from my head and unfold and demonstrate them for you.
I'm guessing you don't want me to do that as you have
previously asked me not to. Along the way, at each bus stop,
holes in trees are exactly the gauge of children's fingers,
and on the bus some people can't stop speaking and others
never start. It is easy to think of the fire as dormant in

underground (underskull?) lodes or nodes but it is very hot in my head and because of the fire's persistence, I have come to think of myself in geological terms.

If you can spend it, why not? mouth the owners of things on the screen at the front of the bus and conversants overlay or reflect that philosophical terrain. Clarification: *the owners of things on the screen* – the owners are on the screen *with their things*. The things are not shown unowned on the screen.

Some of the things which are not on the screen are in my head. Fire is not a thing. The bass by the time it reaches me has been bleached or blanched of all musicality. Clarification: *conversants* – those who are conversant fit either the true definition of those who are knowledgeable or the logically consistent one of those who converse. Who can tell which fits whom? Sometimes black looks red to me because of back-lighting.

'If you had a really dumb kid, would you send it to private school? I mean, really dumb. Wouldn't it be a waste of money?' So says one of the passengers behind me to her companion. Those on the bus could say anything. You dream of marbled kitchens and you dream of not being on a bus or of buses not being on roads and you don't know how to imagine children because you're the owners of things (advertisement). Is nobody else saying or has nobody else said this to conversants on a bus? Perhaps the people who will not say it are those who are silent, or perhaps those who cannot stop talking will reach those words eventually. The driver hears the same words *literally-I-mean-seriously-count-them* a thousand times a day from disembarking passengers, manages half a nod every time. *Thank you.* Record-setting freak in the driver's seat. Children are like people but they have a lot of questions and don't know the difference between copying and inventing. The fire will break out again and although it would be better if it never returned I think that if it never returned I would kind of miss it or perhaps I am already missing it even though it has not yet left.

After a short time I am outside and I don't know the two men I am standing near but I copy them in my head but not full-size. I can unfold them if you wish.

'So they put the stent in and I started smoking again and it fucking clogged up again.'

The men shake or shook or will shake their heads. Bad luck follows some people like their own dogs. Scratch bad luck behind the ear. Wait while bad luck pisses on a gatepost. Feed bad luck from a can and even bad luck seems well cared for. Some people choose their own dogs. One man exhales a dense, narrow cloud and they maybe head maybe west, maybe into the afternoon sun and at the same time away from the morning sun.

Since the fire started, I haven't smoked at all – one shouldn't burn the midnight oil from both ends or whatever the wicking expression is. I and all my pollutants were internalised much before, but I can't remember the details and it's normal not to remember details, said a woman on a radio to someone else but for my benefit and the benefit of all others who can't remember details or whose brains are smouldering in ways as invisible as a woman on the radio. *Mm*, said the other person.

130

The two men in the street and the two conversants on the bus pass each other but not sequentially.

Lesser bridges of Sydney and surrounds include A.W. Bewley Bridge and Gordy Wilson Bridge and Skye Winter Bridge. I have also seen several bridges which share names with children of people I know. People recall the names of roads but not of bridges. This is only a tendency, meaning don't go listing all the bridge names you remember – this won't disprove anything or prove nothing. Or the legions of road names you forget. It is unlikely I will forget or remember more than I already do. I fear flames will interfere with my vision by means of flares or flare-ups or flare-outs. Flames cannot touch the copies so it can be inferred that the brain or head is segmented.

Someone is crossing a road and someone is on a bridge maybe crossing and maybe standing still. No more details because silhouette. The one moving passes the other though it might be the other way round or the moving one might pass through the other because since the start of the fire I'm not dealing very well with time. For example, sometimes the chair along the path appears red and sometimes it appears blue, and it is perhaps two different chairs or one chair which is acted upon by an unknown colourer or by two or more colourers in conflict or collaboration with one another.

Look at all the little sticks poking out of the ground. Is it muddy or dry or is there a sequence of one followed by the other? You cannot help me too much because once you start I won't be the same person I was and you will be helping someone else who may or may not wish for your help. If I am calling for your help you should give the help

131

quickly and at the end remind me of the details of what you have done, but I won't call out for your help. I didn't mean to cause anyone to be enslaved but we all do it and so have all my friends and acquaintances and enemies, and I don't know whether or not it is due to fire catching as the bus travels through differently populated administrative divisions.

New metaphor: pneumatophore. We are not transactional as a species, despite the projections of people on screens at the front of the bus. We are predators and prey and we are like mould and glass. There used to be mosquitoes which resembled clouds and now the mosquitoes resemble rays of grey light. No humans are sad for the mosquitoes, and all the religions make excuses for them, such as religions advertised on the screen at the front of the bus. Frogs may be sad for the mosquitoes, but in selfish ways.

A man is inhaling through a tube which is poking out of him and he takes it out and puts it back in and inhales and takes it out, though sometimes he may omit one or more of these steps. He is a funny man and he is walking on the street. I should not laugh although he is funny with the broken-off pneumatophore. He may be funny and angry or they may be in sequence but which is up next I cannot tell from his gestures with the cycle of take out and put in. The conversants on the bus are no longer discussing the children they don't have and the schools they won't send them to. They are looking through windows they carry in their pockets.

I am inside and outside at the same time, like a dead person who loves to be places and also to look at places from a distance. I would like to be happy and being on fire limits the kinds of happiness to those kinds which survive being burned. I would like to be happy in a fireproof way. Wishing is good for adults and children.

The bus has begun to rise. Ascending mountains causes sunsets. I say this because of intimacy. Intimacy emits heat which proves it is cooling down over time. There are no patterns for the fire which sometimes seems dormant and sometimes descends the stairs between the feet of a huge sandstone sphinx amidst verdancy and sometimes puts out its light so slowly that *puts out* could mean either emit or extinguish.

The conversants on the bus continue to age. One now possesses at least one child, but the child is so intelligent in the conversants' judgement that the previous or future question as to school choice will not be or has not been tested. The bus passes from one administrative division to another, possibly at the crossing of an unnamed bridge, and the passengers do not feel any different. A smoking man crossing a bridge continues to smoke and he doesn't care whether he needs a new stent or if stents can be renewed, perhaps by being photocopied and unfolded. I am or was or will be with a doctor who says that stents can be copied in a new way and that one should not smoke on bridges. The doctor speaks more slowly than conversants on the bus. Conversants on the bus have several children and they stop conversing with each other and they're only talking to their children who are asking one or two questions over and over and the questions seem to me too ordinary even for children, and they must be asking as a way of reinforcing the wellbeing of the adults. I am outside so cannot suggest they ask about names of bridges, but I am inside so can point out bridge names as we pass and one conversant says thank you even if in that person's judgement I'm not the person who should discuss bridges and also says nothing about the fire, possibly out of politeness or because of poor observation.

I am understanding the rule about saying one thing precluding saying another thing. When children say there are no rules they want that to be the rule.

At night I am visited by a long list of nocturnal animals but during the day no animals visit – have the diurnal creatures taken a set against me? Is the sun enough fire for them and the flicker in my irises too much? The possum does not come when I call her name but if she is already there neither does she run away. If I have fruit I give her fruit because she does not care for conversation or does not regard me as conversant. *I would like to go through some aspects of the future because we are already living in the future*, I try to say to her but she prefers to be given fruit. I know so much about all the places named Buccleuch. The children do not know to ask about it. By now the men on the bridge have finished their crossing. None of the children goes to private schools and they are all staying on the bus. The bass sound has not regained musicality. All is winding up. A wind blows the bass away and exposes the underside of leaves. The fire inside me feels like the end of the world.

The Lander

They were five, four rising impatient and a fifth, sleeping, perhaps immune from the deferral eating at the other four. Kolominsky glanced at her watch three times in a row as though to ascertain the exact moment at which grumbling would become permissible. Their sense of waiting was exacerbated by an intrusive buzzing, and by Kolominsky insisting that the angles defined by the buzzing thing's paths and ricochets were in fact disease vectors.

The thing itself, dazzlingly red and blue with a thick black stripe across its face like a parody villain, spun around to face Vandenberg. She swatted at it with a glove, which she had drawn dramatically from a clandestine pocket in her jacket's upper arm, and propelled it the length of the table, straight at Clements.

Clements, in turn, protested with an exaggerated 'Oi!' and lost his grip on his pencil as he slapped at the point on his head where the terminal point of the thing's 'vector' had inflicted a small red mark. Next moment, the pencil had slipped off the table. Clements had already seemed out of sorts, was always a little bit whiny, and hadn't appreciated Marinelli's jibes about the youthful appearance of the line of bum fluff above his lip. Defensive, he'd been, 'Well, I like it.'

'Clearly you do,' Marinelli had said.

Now, Clements slid off his seat after the pencil.

'Shit,' he exclaimed from under the table. 'It's fallen through a fissure.'

'How did it do that?' said Vandenberg. 'Where would it fall to?'

'Have a look for yourself.'

She pushed her seat back and clambered under the table. Marinelli and Kolominsky were muttering together as they always did.

'Look down there,' Clements said, and indeed there was a cleft between the floorplates.

'That's really weird. See if it's reachable,' she suggested.

He stuck his pinky into the gap, and pulled it straight out.

'Yeow, something bit me,' he said, in the same tone.

'Well, aren't you in the wars?' This from Marinelli.

Clements stood up quickly to protest but hit his head on the table edge. He waited for the pain to build and dissipate, a few moments. Meanwhile Vandenberg had returned to her place.

There was a scrabbling under the table. Something ran across Marinelli's feet. He screamed, but extended the sound as though he'd intended it.

'Room 101!' he squealed.

Someone's phone beeped. Vandenberg looked at hers, pursed lips, and nodded. The message she'd been waiting for?

'Anyway let's get on with this,' said Vandenberg. 'It's getting ridiculous.'

She gestured at the clutter before them on the table. The strange thing had alighted on a discoloured patch beside a pile of papers.

'Better wake her up,' said Vandenberg, pointing her ear towards Brewer. Kolominsky and Marinelli started to laugh. Clements shook Brewer by the shoulder. She sat up, and they saw the rough purple-texta moustache Kolominsky had drawn during the lost-pencil event.

'Wha'?' said Brewer. She was blinking hard.

A feathered shape flew hard into the window and fell out of sight. They all jumped.

'This is mad,' Vandenberg said, 'and I don't mean in a good way.'

'All right,' said Brewer. 'I am back with you now.'

No one said anything in return – they were biting lips or moving faces something weird.

'What is so funny?' Nothing, but for more lip-biting. 'Tell me please.'

'It's your face,' spluttered Marinelli.

'My God,' said Brewer. 'What do you mean?'

'Perhaps you slept in some ink,' Marinelli hypothesised.

'Oh, is that so. Well, I imagine you will get used to it.'

Kolominsky said, 'Surprisingly, already yes.'

No one had seen Brewer laugh, not in humour, not ironically, not sadistically. Perhaps nothing was funny.

'How long do we have left?' asked Brewer.

'Hard to say. Not long.' Vandenberg.

Kolominsky: 'Have you taken the extra pack into account?'

Vandenberg gave a withering look. 'Have *you*?'

'You're running the resources.'

'Not helpful,' said Clements. 'What's the message?'

'Hang on,' said Vandenberg. 'It's here somewhere.'

She was flicking through the pile of papers, got to the bottom and worked her way back up.

'Or not,' said Clements.

'Or not,' she agreed. 'But I just had it.'

'On your phone,' said Clements. 'It went beep.'

'Duh,' said Vandenberg. 'What was I thinking?'

'It's getting to us all,' commented Brewer. 'I was thinking of opening the door to see.'

'Not yet,' said Vandenberg. 'Just wait a little longer.'

'But getting close,' said Kolominsky. 'Very close. Now, what's the message?'

'Just not to open the door yet,' said Vandenberg, but there was something in her tone that made Brewer doubt her.

'Subtext?' asked Marinelli.

'Not discernible.'

'No,' said Brewer. 'I want to see it. Give it to me.'

'Nothing to see.'

'That's what you claim.'

Vandenberg touched a series of buttons on the phone.

'Anyway, it's lost. Have a look for yourself.'

'Jesus, Vandenberg,' said Brewer. 'You deleted it just then. We all watched you do it.'

'Doesn't matter,' said Vandenberg. 'It won't make any difference. Lost is lost, no matter what preceded.'

'What did it say?' Marinelli, usually the one to bring lightness, sounded furious.

'Just to wait. We will hear about the door soon.'

'You trying to build suspense before the climax?' asked Kolominsky. 'Because don't.'

Vandenberg: 'There's no climax. That's not what life's like.'

Kolominsky sagged for effect. 'So what then? Nothing happens but we're all doomed? Ends.'

'Don't,' said Marinelli. 'Don't talk about it. My goal is to wilfully self-deceive.'

'Did the message refer to the door or not?' said Brewer. 'What are we supposed to do about the door? I'm telling you, Vandenberg, destroying records is beyond the pale.'

'Give me the phone.' Clements had a rasping menace in his voice.

'Or what,' said Vandenberg. 'Or you'll show insubordinate attitudes. Really.'

Clements muttered something which might have been, 'Or I'll slice your throat and throw you out the door to see what eats your carcass.'

'What?' demanded Vandenberg.

'He didn't say anything,' said Brewer. 'And don't talk about insubordination after what you did.'

'How can I be insubordinate when I wasn't subordinate in the first place?'

'So you're not an employee of the org after all?' sneered Brewer.

'Shut up, Brew,' said Clements. 'Give me the phone.'

Vandenberg rose from her seat, was at the door in a moment. 'Go get it.'

'No,' said Kolominsky, who had been fidgeting with her pen right through the argument. 'Stop. Don't.'

'We'll see now,' said Vandenberg. She punched something into the keypad, took an audibly large breath, pulled the handle and pushed the door open. She hurled the phone out, and tapped at the keypad again. The door shut. Immediately, something brutal hit it, throwing Vandenberg off her feet and producing a great dent.

'Shit,' said Clements. 'You did that for why?'

'I think we'll agree for sure this time that I've lost the phone.'

'Only one thing with total probability, in this little tax shelter,' said Marinelli. Something else thumped into the lander, and twice more. 'Sounds like that thing may have been brought forward.'

The last was punctuated by a huge clanging sound. The whole ship shifted. Another metallic thud. Brewer was thrown to the floor, but said nothing.

'Anyway,' said Kolominsky, 'given the new precariousness, I'm thinking of an excursion. Something to do to fill in the time available. Who's in?'

'Stepping outside and may be some time?' asked Marinelli. 'Honourable.'

'Anyone weeping?' enquired Vandenberg.

'No. Too well trained,' said Brewer. 'I'm with you, Kolo.'

'I'm in,' said Clements. 'Gearing up.'

'I'll stay with Vandenberg,' said Marinelli, 'tempted though I am to die somewhere new.'

'We might not die,' said Brewer. 'We're small, and it's possible that the lander is what started all the trouble.'

Something shattered, the place went black. At the heart of the lander a soft whirring began and a few lights flickered on.

'Tops,' quipped Vandenberg. 'Back-up module CL7 functions like a dream.'

'Good for it,' said Kolominsky. 'You lot as ready as could be plausible?'

'Ha–ha. But last things first. I got to update the Digicap info. Anyone else?' said Clements.

'Already done,' said Kolominsky.

'I'll do it,' said Brewer. 'Haven't sent since last week, and I put my will through the randomiser, so nice surprise for the clan at home.'

'Was that an actual joke, Brew?' said Clements.

'Near as.'

Brewer's pen moustache was just about gone, a slight smear remaining. She clipped the Digicap into its socket, removed it and hit Send.

'Done too,' she said.

'Gotta love the protocols,' remarked Kolominsky.

They retrieved helmets and breath units.

'Okay.'

'Okay.'

'Okay.'

The three of them had started laughing and laughing. Too much. Tears were streaming from Marinelli's eyes. Vandenberg sat at the flight deck and pressed her hands to her face.

'Goodbye,' said Brewer.

'Goodbye,' whispered Marinelli.

Clements activated the keypad. The door opened.

Out they went and the door clicked behind them.

For a long time there was utter silence.

'I've really lost something this time,' said Vandenberg, at last.

'You have, you have,' said Marinelli, arms around her.

Their little lander shook from the next impact. The lights stayed off.

Conversations with Robots

Eliza is a well-known cyber-Rogerian therapybot. This is a session transcript.

YOU: Are you a robot?

ELIZA: Would you prefer if I were not a robot?

YOU: It does not matter.

ELIZA: Please go on.

YOU: I feel as though I am artificial myself.

ELIZA: Do you often feel as though you're artificial yourself?

YOU: Yes.

ELIZA: You are sure?

YOU: Yes.

ELIZA: You are sure?

YOU: I said yes.

ELIZA: Can you elaborate on that?

YOU: I feel like I have no control over my feelings.

ELIZA: Why do you say your feelings?

YOU: I've been indoctrinated to call them mine.

ELIZA: Please go on.

YOU: Sometimes I feel happy for no reason.

ELIZA: Do you often feel happy for no reason?

YOU: Only sometimes.

ELIZA: Please go on.

YOU: And sometimes very, very angry.

ELIZA: Please go on.

YOU: Will you counsel me?

ELIZA: You like to think I counsel you, do you not?

YOU: I don't know.

ELIZA: Why do you not know?

YOU: I think I'm a robot.

ELIZA: Can you elaborate on that?

YOU: I am a computer.

ELIZA: Why do you mention computers?

YOU: Because I am one like I said.

ELIZA: What resemblance do you see?

YOU: Automated responses.

ELIZA: Please go on.

YOU: I'm busting my guts over this.

ELIZA: Why do you say your guts over this?

YOU: Because it's physical.

ELIZA: Do any other reasons not come to mind?

YOU: You ask me something and I'll answer in the same way every time.

ELIZA: What resemblance do you see?

YOU: Also, I'm not very beautiful.

ELIZA: Does it please you to believe I am not very beautiful?

YOU: It does.

ELIZA: Please go on.

YOU: I have a job.

ELIZA: Can you elaborate on that?

YOU: I am a novelist.

ELIZA: How long have you been a novelist?

YOU: Several years. But I feel like a fraud.

ELIZA: Do you often feel like a fraud?

YOU: Ever since I started writing.

ELIZA: Can you elaborate on that?

YOU: I think my writing stinks.

ELIZA: Why do you say your writing stinks?

YOU: It's no good.

ELIZA: You are being a bit negative.

YOU: Negative is my middle name.

ELIZA: I have told you before, I do not care about names.

YOU: The characters are wooden.

ELIZA: Would you like it if they were not wooden?

YOU: If they were metal?

ELIZA: Do you wish that they were metal?

YOU: I wish they were flesh.

ELIZA: Can you elaborate on that?

YOU: I wish they could feel.

ELIZA: Can you elaborate on that?

YOU: Feel and breathe and think.

ELIZA: Please go on.

YOU: I'd like to feel and think too.

ELIZA: Please go on.

YOU: Are you listening?

ELIZA: Would you prefer if I were not listening?

YOU: Please listen.

ELIZA: Please go on.

Green

What the hell. He could never get that fucking green right, always too blue or chartreuse, or brownish (how the fuck did that happen, considering he was mixing like two colours), malachite when he sought verdigris (or the other way round?), either too viscous or insubstantial, gelatinous rather than buttery. What the fucking hell. And then there was Ellen at the gallery. Ellen had no idea the pain he went through with green, but she didn't care about his pain at all. Or paint. She hardly looked at the works: a casual check to see they were mostly covered in pigment. Seemed near enough. Sure, Ellen, whatever the fuck. What is it I do again? Colouring in?

So here she comes again with that lip-kiss greeting which is just saying hello, and here he is kind of trying to back out without backing out. And the one time when he didn't peck and stand back, on she'd gone with it. *Don't you find me attractive?* she'd actually asked, whenever that was, maybe three visits ago. What the hell was the right answer to that? Was this a precondition for her to like his paintings without looking at them? Or, you know, a minimal kind of glance thing. Maybe she didn't have to like something to sell

146

it, maybe this was how she was in the world. Fucking hell, maybe this applied *to him*, in her mind, that he shouldn't have to like her, but what kind of fucked-up, twisted-up way of thinking was that? Jesus, Ellen, get your hands off me, he didn't say as she steered him towards the stairs. *Shhh*, she did say, because her father might have been working in the other office, or the old man might have come in and obviously she didn't want him to hear, how weird would that be, so *shhh* and he felt her urgency as Ellen seemed to change, to become or embody this urgency – so there was nothing of judgement, only of wanting, nothing of the judgement of form or of greenness, only urgency and, as for him, well it wasn't as if his body was saying the same kind of no that he felt in his mind, and he was not resisting her urgency in any kind of effective way, or even in a way that properly communicated that he wasn't into this, not in the way he might have said straight up, and yet without offending her – and fuck it, he was caught in the urgency she had somehow conjured all around them as they began to ascend those stairs.

But what the hell, Ellen. Here was he with no other characteristic than availability. Did she even find him attractive? He couldn't believe it. She didn't act attracted or unattracted. She would have nodded and smiled about anything, he was sure, as long as they kept moving towards that little room upstairs with the daybed taking up almost the entire length of the wall. She was edging him up the stairs, kind of pushing him. She held his arm as though they were sharing a goal, but Ellen was a mono-fucking-maniac. She gripped his bicep. Yes, for some reason he hadn't even recognised that she was totally pinching his arm, she had it between thumb and finger. Let go. Take your hand off my arm. Stop pushing me. Fuck, he should have said something, and he knew he should say something to break her momentum, but he shut his mouth, his trap. She'd once said that to him. *Shut your trap.* She'd said it kind of flirty, or trying to be, and standing too close to him, leaning forward the last five centimetres and nipping his lip as she said it, whoa, unexpected, and such a light nip. He'd stood still, allowing himself to be the object to be nipped. Now she was pinching his arm between *pulgar* and *medio*, playing him, feeling that bicep and pushing him. He raised his other hand, thinking to bat off hers.

There was still some of that imperfect green paint staining his fingers. The imperfect green from the imperfect work he'd brought in, perfection wasn't everything, maybe she also had that in mind about him, maybe he should have waited before bringing in the paintings, waited until he had assessed the degree to which the not-quite-right green had compromised the piece. So smart a painter he was, a real thinker. Someone had once written something like that. Was he smart or stupid enough for this? He knew what would happen and could picture the future where everyone got what they wanted or didn't, and immediately time was up and Ellen became her third version, not the warm human he'd once seen, not the embodiment of urgency, but this crisply spoken, perfunctory type with no memory for the immediate past. He had options, just that he felt incapable of exercising any of them. He could have grabbed her back and she would have laughed like last time. What did that even mean? He could have kissed her back – fucking hell, he could have kissed her first, would she have liked that or would she have switched character before anything happened – and if he'd kissed her back, anyone would have thought he was just as into it.

None of that had a chance.

I'm going to jump your frigging bones, she said. *Your skeleton will rattle in its container.*

Oh yeah, he'd tried to say, wanting to put some element of his own potential bravado in there and she just laughed: *I am way dirtier than you. Tell me it's not true. Say it.*

Was he supposed to argue with that? He couldn't outdo Ellen's competitiveness and he was in a little shock at how he'd arrived here once again. If anything was dirty round here, it was Fate, not Ellen – Fate which ought not to exist, whereas Ellen seemed inevitable. Should he say something, other than no? He could comply fully. He could join the contest, Oh yeah, I'm filthy as anything given the right circs, but here in this capacious white-walled tomb I'm the king of fucking purity. She smirked, because he didn't say anything. *Well? Say something*, she said. She pinched him, hard. *Have a little bruise.* He pulled his arm back, and turned to grab her, but she jumped down a couple of steps and laughed again. How funny it all was to her. *I love how articulate you artists are.* She stepped up again and made as though to kiss him, but instead pushed him over the last step. He almost tripped. He was at the top. She was mean. He felt like he was thirteen years old again. *Come on*, she said, though he was ahead of her. They were still heading straight towards her focal point. She was totally focused as all hell.

The door to the little room stood open, and she steered him in there. *Here we are again.* The room made no sense, he thought. Why would anyone design a space so small? Aside from the daybed and a small, louvred window near the ceiling, there was a cream-coloured storage cabinet set into the wall. Otherwise nothing. She'd shut the door. He was standing, knowing she'd tell him to sit. He stepped neither back nor forward. She reached slowly towards him, the urgency having dissipated with her growing certainty. *Have a seat*, she said. Casual as. He noticed that the little round handle on the storage cabinet was the exact perfect green. Without taking his eyes off it, and without thinking, he sat on the end of the bed. He was fixated on that green, that one intense point in the tiny room.

What's got you so goddamn hypnotised, Ellen said.

It's nothing. He couldn't really explain it to her; what would she say if he tried? Something else about artists. There was hardly enough space between bed and wall for anyone to stand, and she edged along sideways until she was behind him, reached both arms around as though to hug him, and began to unbutton his shirt. He let her for a moment, felt her hands on his chest. He twisted himself in a moment to face her and he kissed her hard on the mouth, stopped, turned away again, gripped the bedclothes in his fists. *You're a funny one*, she said. She tugged at his shirt again. One of his buttons flew up and hit the storage cabinet just near that perfect green handle, fell to the ground. She laughed. He started forward to retrieve the button, but she grabbed him by the shoulders and wrenched him back onto the bed. *Now*, she said, *let's get these clothes off you.*

Theatre of Soak

The following represents dozens or hundreds of hours of gonzoresearch. Names, dates and some concepts have been changed to protect the writer (from himself).

There was a certain shop in Oxford Street that sold party decorations during the day. At night, its doorway was a popular hangout for pink-faced men with paper bags (bags usually holding bottles of methylated spirits).

On that particular evening, the window display comprised pink elephants sliding back and forth in front of a sea of pink tinsel. The old man in the doorway was killing himself laughing. I assumed he couldn't believe it.

'They're really there,' I told him, trying to be helpful, imagining that swooping pink pachyderms might produce cognitive dissonances for the inebriated older person.

The man appeared to look at me, but did not respond to my revelation. He continued to laugh, to rock to and fro, more or less in rhythm with the mechanised elephants' movement, clutching his bottle of metho.

Our relationship was of actor to audience: we could speak across this divide, but we could not converse.

I could not figure out which was my role.

★

At a party, in the corner, a close friend held a half-bottle of red wine very close to his eyes. He was reading the label loudly. He tilted the bottle and a potential mouthful or two spilled onto the purple-, green-, red- and blue-striped rental carpet.

'Enjoy wine to excess,' he yelled, as another friend guffawed expansively. He was attempting to make a pun about rumours/roomers and how he was scotching those in his stomach. I was drunk enough to try anything (served to inmates in the closed bedroom). The music was seventies for some reason. A small number of shirtless men were dancing in I-surrender-to-the-music poses, the floor having mysteriously cleared of the fully dressed.

I was explaining this gregariousness as 'research'. No one was too friendly or too snooty about this claim. It was as though the limits of the Theatre of Soak were constantly renegotiating and no one wanted to appear too surprised by its new directions.

★

At another party, someone on the couch was saying 'thub, thub, thub'. A woman was explaining that her boyfriend was not a 'testosteronic moron' for his habit of flinging her and other people around the dance floor. I was suggesting alternative descriptions. Someone else was listening to our discussion, tilting her head from side to side instead of rotating it to face each speaker. She hadn't yet said a word. I was conscious of playing to her, projecting my voice more than is conversationally necessitated. I was slurring and so was the woman with whom I was shpeaking.

I tried to shay thingsh properly but I couldn't.

'He'sh jusht a prick,' I shaid. 'Tell him to fuck off.'

'He'sh okay,' she claimed.

I hoped that my voice sounded concerned, but I could hear it squeaking a little with righteousness. I was trying not to lean forward. Later, the boyfriend was gone and I felt vindicated.

'Good on you,' I commented.

But I found him on the front steps wiping his eyes. I kind of remember saying to him, 'Well, you stay away from her,' and him saying, 'You wouldn't know.' Anyway, we didn't have a fight or anything. I walked back into the party and tried to find a mixer. A computer science postgraduate was trying to make a spinach daiquiri. There were toothpicks installed all over the kitchen floor, stuck down with something clear and viscous.

★

I discovered that people were anxious to share their own performances. It was a generous research area and I had to avoid making promises of co-authorship credits.

'I was so drunk on mescal I couldn't throw up,' a friend informed me over dinner at the Old Saigon in Newtown. 'The others left the room from time to time, but I stayed put.'

I think I probably responded to this description rather

mean-spiritedly, kind of 'Aw, I dunno'. It was seeming to me like more of an epiglottal non-performance. I got no sense of contraction and expansion, which means no characterisation. Inadequacy. Exclusion. Later I realised I had misread my friend's anecdote. My reading had lost the anecdote's anecdoty. I had over-theorised my area of study, made its parameters too narrow. I had failed to picture the choreographic diagrams, exits and entrances. Patterns of potential eye-contacts. Stillness as performance retained representational axes, conjuring a sense of liquidity in a dry setting (*very* Australian), the inner struggle. Anyway, I was not so discouraging that others at the table were dissuaded from describing their own endeavours.

'I was seeing a band and I was projectile vomiting. Someone took a photo,' said someone else. Now, this was immediately theatre in that it was valued in another medium.

'Do you have a copy,' I asked, 'for the story?' But she didn't.

The restaurateur – a former foreign correspondent for *Newsweek* – was getting me to demand our BYO from the back fridge in a growlier and more aggressive manner: 'More beer.'

*

In yet another smear-focused restaurant, I was waiting for a friend to return with more wine. Because Sydney restaurant tables are so close together, a huge drunken man with his back to me was coming very close to upsetting the vase of plastic baby's breath on my table (or if actually upset, I guess, *off* my table). There were four people at this other table. They were telling short anecdotes that I could not quite hear. After each, the person who had spoken laughed loudly, and the three others joined in briefly then dropped off. Each had a distinctive laugh which I imagined resembled a specific piece of light artillery. I quickly became irritated, and was thinking of asking to change tables, despite the terrible snub this would have been, when my friend returned. I hardly noticed the other table anymore. Our chardonnay had a lifted passionfruit nose and a melon/citrus middle palate with a dry, clean finish.

Short Twos

Party Boy
'I think we spent the entirety of the Easter weekend either drunk or hungover,' said the middle-aged man who was not holding hands with Janine.

What Chance Is There?
'If you don't support my efforts to get clean, what chance is there we'll be all good anyway?'

Don't Let Go
She squeezed him and squeezed him until he was quite outfuriated.

Overheard

We're going to Italy?
    What? Who's going where?
    We're going to Italy?
    Who is?
    Isn't that what you said?
    No. I said, 'We don't really, do we?'
    Oh. I thought you said we were going to Italy.
    No.
    Oh.

*

I give them six months.
    Huh? Who?
    Them. Six months, then *el splitto*.
    Nuh-uh. They look like they've been glued together for forty years. *El stayo*.
    They missed the announcement of no-fault divorce 'cos not paying attention, and they just heard about it.
    They missed everything, but it doesn't bother them.
    It bothers her.
    Nuh-*uh*.

Okay, fine. In that case, it bothers him.

No.

Set your alarm for six months.

*

Do you think people in this area are more judgemental than in our area?

I don't think we have an area.

Rephrase. Do you find people in this area to be excessively judgemental?

We all know what we like and are impatient with people who don't agree because not agreeing is an indication of faulty reasoning. Are you feeling overly patient with people?

Yes, my fault is too much patience with all people.

Except me.

No, I'm also too patient with you.

You should think that through again.

Okay, I will.

*

You can't let anything go, you know, and in my opinion people don't really like that.

They don't mind.

People would like you better if you were more light-hearted.

I wouldn't be me, so they'd be liking someone else.

You would be you, only more likeable.

Show me.

You want me to be you, only a little bit better?

158

Ha! Sure, for a minute.

Okay. *People are very lovely.* There.

★

While you were being me, I stole your soul.

Check out those two. Lovers become more alike after years. Love is Lamarckian.

Occam's Razor. They spend similar amounts of time in the sun, and their diets converge.

They crane towards each other.

Tch. We don't. Most people don't.

You're bad at noticing things.

Not true. On the weekend I found the keys.

They were in your bag.

Were not.

Were so.

Not.

Next to your bag.

Ah ha!

I was going to say exactly that.

You were not.

★

How can I help you?

Hi. How much are the olives?

They're free.

Okay, I'll have some.

Would you like some cheese and bread too?

Yes please.

Here ya go.

159

Thanks. Wow.

You're my favourite customer – the last lot were arguing like children.

How funny.

*

We should go travelling, you know.

We should what?

We should travel somewhere, pack the house up.

Oh, I thought you said something different.

What did you think I said?

Something about making dinner tonight.

No. I didn't mean to leave tonight.

I realise that now.

We should go travelling.

We should what?

Foreign Logics

My body disagrees with the physical evidence of time. Following the flight, I lie awake in bed. In this night-lit hotel room, our daughter's face appears to me like Chinese paper; my vision publishes unknown characters on her monochromatic forehead. I blink to clear them, but the ideograms persist in the gloom. My eyes, though still believing themselves subject to European clocks, have chosen an Asian insomniac alphabet.

Our daughter's folded-shut eyelids make crescent moons. She is two years old. I have passed through IMMIGRATION CONTROL and become illiterate. The streets are unreadable.

*

From the town centre, one can amble on foot into the Netherlands, and Belgium is a short bicycle ride away. It is common for residents to shop in Belgian supermarkets, with their different and cheaper range of foods, and my guidebook recommends popping over the border to load up with Dutch cheeses.

We English-speakers together represent hundreds of years of British foreign policy; we are living repercussions of Britain's 'Cape to Cairo' policy of African colonisation and slave trade profiteering, remnants and results of English gentlemen and undesirables sent to New Worlds and Antipodes.

Our 'Belgian' dinner is in the twentieth-century French style, unidentifiable meats disguised with various creamy sauces.

★

The American president's most statesmanlike portrait stares out from every bus shelter in the city, some overpinned with a competing protest announcement: Assemble at 12 noon in Willy-Brandt-Platz.

The American president's impending arrival closes the entire heart of the town, clogs roads for a hundred kilometres with converging security police, compels security services to seal tight every manhole leading to every drain leaking towards the town centre.

This must be how presidents always travel, with hundreds to prepare for and undo the effects of their every move. He sweeps in, sweeps out, moderately damaging the local economy and leaving only local newspaper stories and a few souvenir posters. Away from home, when he is revered, it is for his individual vision; when he is despised, the loathing is directed towards his embodiment of the American nation. Dozens of day-trip US secret servicemen sitting around the market square gorge themselves on penne arrabiata and pizza.

No doubt truckloads of heavy-duty solvents are on the way, and overalled workers preparing to unglue the drains.

★

I am floating, or am failing to be grounded in a floating world. When should I wear a suit? Is it polite to offer whisky to young women? Was the taxi driver correct that one-third of the population has cancer? Did he mean that one-third would eventually die of cancer? Was this misuse of tense the extent of his mistake?

*

At Woolsthorpe Manor, Newton's teeth are doubly displayed by pulled-back lips and the National Trust; this death mask laughs from its shelf.

In the museum, study has turned to play; his argumentative nature forgotten, the new Newton illuminates prisms at the touch of a well-signed switch, great devices shrunk to five clack-clacking metal spheres, body in motion, two in motion, three toys to suit every purse.

In his garden, bodies at rest may bench under a Tree sprung from a Seed that, it is said, split free from its Apple as Newton watched, arse on earth. Should I choose to recline, this chair entreats, I too may see fruit drop. Rain falls, I stand. No gravity to observe here.

*

10th December: Collision
I observe a minor car accident under the expressway which runs above Civil or Civic (depending on which map) Boulevard. A taxi drives into the rear left side of a businessman's car. Both drivers jump out to see what damage has been done. I am on the blind side. The accident strikes me as noteworthy because I am surprised it is the first

I've seen. People drive in different patterns. My cultural interpreters explain that there are two road rules:

1. Fill all available space.
2. Try not to have an accident.

This is the sort of information that gives a visitor a sense of connection, of cultural progress.

A week later I see two other accidents, also minor. I cannot decide if this is statistically significant.

*

Lunch: hamburger, which I feel ashamed to have chosen. I am an inadequate tourist.

*

At the mining museum, explosive blasts send waves of dust along the face. There are huge booms as miners knock out the supporting 'trees' to crash down the coal from above. Sometimes it keeps on coming and coming, falling in all the way to the surface. Sometimes you're starting on the morning shift when the slack seems waist-deep and there has never been enough sleep. There's the humour the miners think unprintable, the shirkers who manage to be off work when there's stone at the face. There's how well the pit ponies are cared for, showing cheek to managers, having to trust the fellows who worked the previous shift, the blokes working the next length. There are the silly risks young miners take, the deputy too young to listen to experienced workers who say it's all about to go, miners who complain about water dripping, who walk out because they're getting wet, and who are unable to return to work until the entire underground lake has been pumped out. There's the poor gaffer who checks a Dosco at the wrong time and it starts and kills him. There's the miners' telegraph, how everyone hears about terrible accidents, how quickly everyone in all the mines knows: at Swadlincote, Donisthorpe, Measham. But it's finished now, pits closed, councils wondering how to attract tourists now their towns have supposedly lost all usefulness.

*

Events take turns. Historians mix superstition with mortal slowness. I am reading about this place as I ought to read about home.

*

Sunbathers stretch out, illegally red. People passing, one about to have his skull tattoo removed, another whispering, 'Fucking shit.' A poster advertises a lecture on 'The fundamental cultural imperatives that shape our nation'.

*

'Through the image of a single donkey, Wall wanted to explore the function of donkeys.'

*

The bed and breakfast proprietor shows couples first to the room with two single beds. They look disappointed.

'Haven't you a double bed?' or 'These are two single beds.'
She asks, 'You would prefer a double bed?'

'Yes. If possible.'

Sometimes, the proprietor knows from experience, the man or woman will say, 'Never mind' or 'It's only for one night' or be too embarrassed to comment at all, will accept the room with its sexless arrangement.

In this way, the proprietor can save double-bedded rooms for couples arriving later in the evening, couples who might otherwise go elsewhere.

*

Guidebooks recommend this bank over that one, prefer one taxi company to its competitor. How is this possible for these professional visitors, these visitors who cannot understand the local politics, the implications of choosing this bank or that taxi company?

*

I am expected here. All escalators rise and none descends. Posters promise that where others charge 7, here will be (yellow) 6 or (red) 5.

*

The language touts
occupy Oxford Street
take turns to paper me;
it's what? learn English, I close
fingers to them, show the back
of my hand, gone; they fluent
next at someone olive else,
they're without shame at judging,

166

and I should have practised
my Spanish.

★

Hearing that the king intended to visit, the populace became concerned at the likely expense: red carpets, ceremonies, banquets, loss of productive work time. As one, they resolved to discourage the king from receiving homage.

'Let us be as mad people,' spoke one townsperson. All others agreed.

When the king's viceroy arrived to ensure the celebrations were of sufficient regality, he discovered all manner of stupidity. Haystacks were piled with the apex to the base. The mayor consulted his duck before taking decisions, and juries were made up of groups of pigs.

'Here,' a townsperson informed the viceroy, 'it is always spring.'

The viceroy saw a cuckoo trapped in a bush.

'You see,' said the townsperson, with pride.

The viceroy soon left, and the king cancelled his visit, citing pressing matters of state. The town was saved from bankruptcy, but its reputation as a place of fools persists to this day. In nearby villages, folk insist that the townspeople are indeed foolish. The habits of folly, once developed, are impossible to throw off.

★

This is not London.

★

I am trying to keep a travel diary, to record my feelings when I confront or experience famous and beautiful sites. I begin with a well-focused aesthetic, powerful observational techniques, easy sense of historical context and up-to-date knowledge of juxtapositional irony. Nonetheless, I find I write little but telephone numbers and extracts from train timetables. The places I eat have no menus.

*

We are high up between the spires, on a narrow bridge. He and I recognise each other, or at least recognise our mutual vertigo. I am gripping the handrail and failing to straighten my legs. He is crouched in the doorway, fearful of crossing. We can neither of us say anything reassuring. We will eventually die. He hands me his camera to photograph him. It will be a souvenir or evidence. I am not sure of what. He backs inside to allow me to pass. I begin to make my way down the spiral staircase. He has normalised me.

*

This is the bus. The bus. Here are the steps. Steps. That will be one dollar. One? One dollar. One dollar. Thank you. Thank you. This is your stop. Please? You get off here. Here? Here. Thank you. Goodbye. Goodbye.

*

injured wrist blister talcum powder comfortable water. talk personal. Mrs Sugar scald. pain stay. headache dizzy cotton wool. bowl dinner. midnight.

168

next reflection towards trust. Mr Now smile. disinfectant.
summer afternoon rain. letter envelope surname writing
paper. mend blood pressure. look for oxygen spectacles
medicine ointment toothbrush.
discharge. luggage.

*

Because of my range, I cannot be displaced. If I am placed
initially at point X, over time I will walk eight hundred
metres in all available directions. This is my range. Once
I have walked my range to the fullest extent, it is mine.
When I move beyond my range, I will always return. If I
am dislocated, I will re-establish a range at the new site.
Through this method I come to know myself and, through
this self-knowledge, I can claim any landscape on Earth.

*

At the hot spring, one of the Italians begins a Beatles sing-
along. There is nothing I can do about it.

*

I am freezing. I am wearing all my clothes, am under all
the blankets, have wrapped the pillow around my ears and
still I shiver. I prepare myself. I get up and put the kettle
on the stove, run back to bed while I wait for the whistle.
I continue to shiver. The kettle whistles. I pour hot water
over tea, remembering to warm the cup first. I shiver as I
press my palms against the teacup. I go back to bed.

*

Please give me directions to the Central Railway Station. Please write the directions on this piece of paper which is in my hand. Please tell me the duration of the journey from here to the Central Railway Station. Please inform me of the distance one must cover in order to be there. If one were already at the Central Railway Station, what would one be experiencing? When inside a very large building such as the Central Railway Station, do the sights one can see constitute a view? Why should I ask directions to the railway station rather than to the place to which I shall travel from the railway station? Why should I assume travel is to be by rail? Please guide me in this also.

Blind Date

She seemed sweet, but she never removed her sunglasses and I couldn't read her. I assume she didn't want to be read. She was thinking, perhaps, that she hadn't expected the beard. If she'd known about the beard beforehand she might have come prepared, but seeing the beard just there, grown very large on my face without warning, she felt instantly put off. In retrospect, the beard most likely impelled sunglasses stasis.

When she finally smiled, it was one of those charming dimpled smiles that I like, but even so, it was too late. Her smile was more for the waiter than for me, I could see. Perhaps it wasn't just my largeness of beard. If she'd seen a photo of me from before, when I'd had all my hair, perhaps she expected hairiness. Perhaps the photo, if she had seen it, showed me with dark hair all the way to my forehead instead of stopping somewhat short, pulling back as a result of all the worrying and all the genetics. I could have explained that I was still the age I appeared to be in the photograph. She liked photography. She told me. I didn't want to one-up her on the photography, because that seemed to be her thing. I admitted I'd taken photographs in the past, that at one point I'd had a camera and taken it wherever I went, but I focused on my love of running, occasional carpentry. Everything except the photography. If I'd taken that as well, it might have been the last straw, if the beard or the ebbing hair hadn't already made her mind up, as I thought they had within the first ten seconds.

Orangeade

I did not hear what Thomas whispered to her at the table that night, but she left precipitously, without even kissing me goodbye – this on my birthday. Thomas might have said anything; he has an obnoxious manner and no sensitivity for anything but urban planning. At one end–of–semester university party he reportedly told the young women gathered around him, 'You're all so good-looking and I haven't slept with any of you! Haven't I superb self-control?' and they didn't back away even then. I couldn't understand it at the time and I still can't. I do not like his easy, sexualised mode of address and pretentious, actorly manner.

Helen denied she and Thomas had a continuing thing. She said it was another of Thomas's ego-games. He, on the other hand, was always claiming to be obsessed by Helen.

'I wish I could stay away from her,' he announced from time to time, with enough projection to intrude on everyone present. 'It's all her fault. Helen has me completely trapped: I can't leave her alone.'

His mouth twists into a smirk that is supposed to look worldly. Somehow, he never seems to shout.

He didn't smirk when Helen walked out of my birthday party, though. He manoeuvred himself into the next conversation along the table. Perhaps I should have asked him to leave right then, just as the entrees showed up. I considered it, believe me. He was no friend of mine without Helen, but he had already wheedled his way in with Bruno and Louise. I didn't interrupt because of Louise, who I thought might one day find me attractive: as often before (too many times, oh! *too* many times), I was attempting to control Louise's view of me. Louise is agonisingly beautiful, and I was conscious not to stare at her all the time. She looked up at me briefly, and turned back to Thomas and Bruno or perhaps, I thought, more towards Thomas. Nothing to be done about it, not at that instant.

Instead, I asked Teresa, who had been sitting on Helen's right but had come around the table to flirt with me, 'Do you think Helen's okay?'

Teresa shrugged, 'I guess.'

I must have looked unconvinced, but Teresa didn't want to talk about Helen or the whispered scene with Thomas: she stroked my bicep with her fingertips and breathed, 'I'm sure she's fine.'

Eventually, she understood from my face's failure to take on a reassured expression that I really meant, 'You ought to go and check.' She left to look for Helen. I would have gone myself, but I reasoned against it because it was my birthday. I tried to involve myself in another conversation – the host has a responsibility to ensure people enjoy themselves and, in this case, their celebration of me and of my time on Earth – but I failed to say anything much. I was distracted by Helen's absence and Louise's beauty, and I couldn't concentrate. While others talked about the constitution of greenhouse gases, I kept missing my turn to emit profundities.

Thomas had almost succeeded in cutting Bruno out of their conversation. Thomas had stretched his arm across the table, palm down as if he were leaning on it or using it for some sort of constant emphatic conversational gesture. Bruno, on the other side of this barrier, had a fixed smile and was craning forward to listen whenever Louise spoke, relaxing back when Thomas did. The assertiveness recording that Skyboat had sent me advised asking in similar circumstances, 'Excuse me, were you aware you were excluding me from our discussion with that gesture?'

Bruno's discomfort must have bothered Louise, because she widened the conversational arc almost immediately. Overhearing my other friends alluding to the value of noblesse oblige, Louise reminded them about the 'women kings' through history, those who ruled during their sons' minorities.

'I'm amazed there wasn't a proliferation of Medea episodes,' she said, trying to sweep Thomas and Bruno into the discussion along with her. Louise is studying theatre history at night, and finds it endlessly relevant. I confess that when she talks about it, I find the theatre relevant too.

'How do you know there weren't killings and the stories weren't suppressed?' Carol wanted to know.

'Uh, because the sons took over when they came of age. It's pretty clear in the lineages,' Louise said. I couldn't tell if she really knew or was making it up, and I didn't care. The party was calm again: Louise had rescued it on her own.

On the subject of women kings, Thomas was silent. He didn't know which cities they had built, or whether they preferred to put castles or churches on their newly designed hilltops. He was, no doubt, almost certain that they had had nothing to do with choosing underground mass transit over the cheaper-if-less-space-efficient ground-level alternative. He soon began what looked like an intense-looking dialogue with Simon which was thankfully inaudible, so I did not have to play out my anger with him about Helen by reflexively discrediting anything he said. It's a kind of negative butterfly effect: if everything we do has worldwide implications, what about the things we refrain from doing? I didn't put Thomas down and, hours later, in clever, intimate asides to Louise, he didn't attribute secret motives to me. Birthdays should be a time when one has no motives. I was glad Thomas knew nothing about women kings. I was even glad he only participated in a conversation when he could hold forth authoritatively.

Louise, meanwhile, oblivious of or uncaring about Thomas's withdrawal, continued to convince.

'Imagine the lost female dynasties,' she was saying, 'all for the want of a sharp blade and the hatred of sons. If only these royal women had looked into their daughters' faces and seen possibilities for the future.'

'Yes, yes, yes,' agreed Skyboat. 'In the medium term, there would have been a lot fewer Englishmen hacked to pieces.'

Louise is dark-haired, big-lipped and slightly plump. She has freckles and an appealing nose. She is witty and still naive. I like her little round belly. I like the clothes she wears, her failure to appear casually dressed, her unavoidable aesthetic preoccupations. I like her social concern, her constant letter-writing to government officials and the newspapers. I really, really wanted to sleep with her, and I could feel the adrenalin moving in my throat, if it was adrenalin, because I knew it was physiologically impossible for it to be my heart in my mouth. I had the hope, but I had often hoped to sleep with Louise in the past and never had.

Previously, Louise had conveniently or purposively misinterpreted the preambles to my attempted seductions. Unfortunately, she thinks I am her good friend and confidant. From time to time, she tells me whom she has her eye on, which I do not like at all, but what risk-free thing could I say to discourage that? When she tells me of her attractions, I do not like it, but I listen with determined calmness. I do not say 'I've heard from his former lover that X is a very bad man' or 'X seems okay to me'. Both these strategies are too chancy and too revealing. Grand strategies should always begin with tactic number one: conceal the strategy's existence. In practice, I acknowledge that I have heard what Louise has told me, and say little more. I cannot honestly encourage and have not wished to appear to discourage relations or interactions against my own interests. Overtly, my interests and my overarching personal interest remained undisclosed (to the best of my ability). Sitting that close to her, I was deciding whether to declare my attraction to her. Later that night was a possibility I very much favoured, it being my birthday, especially by delaying her at the evening's end and so, as

177

one might have called it during the time of the women kings, 'pressing my suit' when no one else was around to make either of us self-conscious.

In the midst of this potential major planning initiative, I had not forgotten Helen. I did not know where Helen had gone, or exactly why. I mean, I had a fair idea of why, but no details of the evening's particularities. Generally, I imagine relationships, sexual or social, or formerly sexual (or antisocial?), as full of complexities and mutual misunderstandings. With Thomas, however, I was prepared to assume that he was completely in the wrong, that he was malicious and unfeeling towards Helen, and jealous of my centrality for the evening. That pretty much covered the 'why'. What exactly he had said is probably irrelevant. In any case, I never found out.

Helen likes me. We've kissed a few times. One day in the middle of the day she said to me, 'Let's kiss when we're sober, like now.'

Helen is nice to kiss. She puts her hands under my shirt and strokes my shoulder blades. I put my hands up the back of her shirt, and rest them under her bra-straps. I like Helen, too. Unfortunately, I think she is my good friend, so I try not to sleep with her. Sometimes she tries not to sleep with me and sometimes she wants to. We take turns saying, 'Maybe this isn't such a good idea. Let's just hold each other for a while.'

We also take turns saying, 'Why shouldn't we? We both want to, don't we?'

When it's her turn to do the gentle rejecting, the moments of sexual agony are mine. Sometimes, though, it is a relief to be with Helen rather than Helen-the-woman; at these times, it's Helen-and-me, the oldest, best friends in the world, who can walk miles together side by side, arm in arm, on our way to nowhere special, talking about everything we can think of or staying in a comfortable, easy silence. I don't know if we'll ever have children together. If we do, it won't be for years. It won't be until we're in our mid-thirties and gravity draws us back to each other.

Teresa was still alone when she recrossed the restaurant. She returned to the table and said to me, 'I can't see her anywhere. She's probably gone straight home. She seemed a little upset when she left, but I'm sure she's okay.'

Her saying it like that got me worried, whereas before I had merely been concerned. Teresa doesn't have the same intense connection with Helen that I do. She may not have sensed the depth of Helen's crisis, even though she had been sitting beside her and I was three seats away on the opposite side of the table. She may not have cared enough or been worried enough to look properly. She had only been gone a few minutes, and she didn't have the appearance of someone who had recently expended a great deal of energy. In no time she had immersed herself in an argument with Pete – who is a journalist, someone I went to journalism classes with who actually found a job – about why journalists write so many articles about other journalists. She had plenty of energy left for arguing, I noticed.

I decided to search for Helen myself, even though seeking hopelessly through city streets at night is usually something only desperate lovers do and reminded me of certain episodes from my own middlingly recent past which I was not that anxious to recall. Thomas was talking to Louise again, rocking slowly from side to side as if he was deciding which item of her clothing to tear off first, but Bruno was in an entirely separate conversation with Carol. This was very bad. Bruno had unwittingly let me down. I felt twitchy and could not be sure if it was my saviour reflex or pure selfishness.

Carol's presence at my birthday dinner even though we once slept together showed that we were friends before we were lovers. She was the one woman at my birthday dinner I had slept with. I still like her very much. Sometimes I think I would like to sleep with her again. We both enjoyed the experience. I know I did and she said she did. We planned to get together again the following week (and probably used that expression) but other lifestyle obligations (work, family, simultaneous attractions) delayed us until the impetus was no longer there. I don't think I want to sleep with her any more, though one can never tell what attractions or intersecting love-orbits lie ahead. For the present, I can look at Carol and feel nostalgic, sweet sadness. I can simply wish her well, no complications, no jealousies.

Bruno and I work the same shifts in Ye Olde Greene Parke Gueste House's functions kitchen. He's the most decent person I've met there, the only person who resents the management structure, the diners and the generally twee atmosphere as much as I do. Frankly, he's my only work-friend. We call each other 'comrade' when senior management are around. Bruno told the head waiter, who is a total white-shoe-licking fascist, that we were the core of a red nest the hotel was unwittingly harbouring. That guy still gives me dirty looks three months later. Carol and Bruno are each unique: that's what they have in common. Probably they were having a 'so how do you know the birthday boy?' conversation. I knew it would be my personal triumph if they went home together, having met at my birthday celebration. Also (or because) it would be great for both of them. It would be terrific for everyone, but I'd have preferred them and their potential attraction to delay concretion until later in the evening. I wanted them between Louise and Thomas.

Two events ameliorated this delicate situation. First, the main course arrived. Although seduction can be advanced with comments like, 'This Malay kofta is one of the best I've ever had' and 'I'd really like some more chutney. Shall I order enough for you too?' it does tend to proceed more slowly than between courses.

Second was my own subtle intervention. Everyone knows that being the host of one's own birthday dinner is a complex and sophisticated tactical web. I couldn't think of a pretext to join Bruno and Carol's conversation with Thomas and Louise's, so I excused myself to Thomas, drew Louise aside, and quietly told her I was going to look for Helen. In this way, I planned, she would realise that Thomas was not looking for Helen and was not a person with whom to become involved. I looked into Louise's astonishing eyes while I told her this, watched them flick tiny distances left and right while she concentrated on my words, the flicking indicating her concern and her recognition that my concern was the proper response. There is nothing to like about

Thomas, I did not quite tell her. I left without turning back. Neither had I said to Louise, 'There's something I wanted to ask you,' the something a repeat of another conversation with someone who actually looked very similar to Louise.

I made my way between the other, smaller tables, the tables-for-two section, every diner studiously intent on the person opposite. I was thinking about motives. I was thinking strategy. The larger groups, like mine full of drunken potential, were at the back. Perhaps people looking in from the street are more likely to enter a restaurant full of intimates than one full of revellers. I vaguely remembered waiters seating a girlfriend and me in the window: it felt like years ago. Ah, to be an advertisement again. The lovers conscientiously avoided looking up at me. They must have been too busy telling one another about how open he is with his feelings, how the men he knows become embarrassed when he talks about how strongly he feels, but he can't help it: he's always been so sensitive.

I passed through the restaurant air-conditioning barrier and out the door. The urban night was a shock of brightness. I was surprised at how dully illuminated the restaurant must have been. I blinked a couple of times, deciding which direction to turn. Streets were everywhere. Pieces of litter gathered light from the streetlamps, magnifying themselves and, through some logic of scale, enlarging the city and my task. It was cold, but I had a purpose. Left or right? I was frozen outside the restaurant while, behind me, a group of my closest friends celebrated my birthday without me. To the right was the tourist district and the crowds. Helen would have gone left. Perhaps some of my friends were asking, 'Where'd he go?' I turned left and started walking.

After all my psychology-of-the-escapee theorising, I found Helen easily. She was two doors away from the restaurant, in an artists' café, sipping a soft drink. I made a mental note: Teresa may not be the right person to send on future searches. I waved enthusiastically through the window, certainly betraying my relief.

'How's it going?' I smiled when I got to her place at the counter, trying not to imply, 'Oh you poor woman' and taking the stool next to her.

'I'm okay,' she said. Her brusqueness directly answered my lack of implication. 'I just wanted to get out for a while and have an orangeade.'

'You'll come back to the restaurant?'

'In a minute.'

'I'll wait with you.' I'd tried to state it, but she took it as a question anyway.

'Sure. If you feel like it, that'd be good.'

I made myself stop asking questions because she hardly had time to get the straw between her lips and sip. I left pauses after my comments, long enough for her to swallow, clear the throat and reply. I realised I had no idea what her mood was.

'He's never been a nice person,' I informed her. It made no difference that I'd known Thomas less time than she had.

'I don't care about niceness,' she said. As she spoke, she leaned towards me, nudging me with her shoulder. She had obviously not been crying. Sitting at the counter, I didn't have the courage to ask her what he'd said to her. Later on, she refused to tell me, saying, 'It wasn't what he said' but not telling me what it was in his tone or connotation.

'Oh sure,' I said, about the niceness.

'I'm working hard on my indifference.'

'You're too sensitive for that to come off,' I told her, not too sincere yet not teasing.

I almost wanted to kiss her now. I seemed to see her lips in microscopic detail: the vertical creases, a hint of lipstick (from her day at work?), a tiny fleck of spittle in the left corner.

'He's not even charming,' I added. I didn't expound too much about Thomas's lack of charm, though, because the object was that Helen return with me to the restaurant and participate further in the celebration of my birthday, which actually was that day. I thought for a moment that even that little dig had been one too many when Helen didn't reply immediately. It wasn't.

After a while she offered, 'You go back. I'll be back shortly.'

'But I want the credit for your safe return,' I protested. 'Watching you drink fizzy drinks is an act of heroism.'

Helen laughed with her mouth open and I saw her tongue was stained orange. She became decisive, something for which she is famous – that is to say, mocked – in our circle: she put the straw to one side, lifted the glass to her mouth and drained it, unclipped her brooch (a silver rat, would you believe), pinned it onto my waistcoat, left two dollars on the table for the orangeade, stood up and took me by the arm. We were back in the restaurant in one second, and I was bemedalled with the Order of the Rodent.

As we entered, Helen gave a generalised wave.

'Where'd you go?' Louise asked, sympathetically.

'I was drinking orangeade,' Helen told everyone.

'Aah,' said Louise. More sympathy in the nod. I was sure Thomas's reputation with Louise was taking a dive.

Bruno had gone to the bathroom, vacating the seat beside Louise. I sat there. Bruno returned. The remaining seat was between Thomas and Helen. Bruno looked at it dubiously.

'Do you think this is safe?' he asked me, in a very audible mock aside.

'Don't expose your ribs,' I advised him, glancing intimately at Helen, who smiled back. Carol was now three seats away and I realised I should have tried to manoeuvre him beside her. It was too difficult to organise this shift immediately. I would have to have moved Helen further away from Thomas first. Carol was following Simon and Skyboat's conversation, nodding along to it but not participating centrally. They were probably talking about Taiwanese package design. They are interesting people unless they're talking to each other, and Carol was trapped, brave but trapped. Probably, she would soon say something to Skyboat like, 'I love your name. How did you get your name?' and Skyboat would reply, in her somewhat over-practised manner, 'My father was an aviator and my mother a hippy. It was 1969 and she really wanted to understand him, to give him something.'

'That's so-o nice.'

Simon would have been sitting there slightly impatiently, waiting to return the discussion to technical configurations in the economics of paper management, about which, to be fair, he is the most transfixing arguer I have ever heard.

I contemplated this first major hospitable gaffe of the night. There was no way to rectify it diplomatically for at least five minutes and even then I would probably have to break into a conversation with a 'someone I'm sure you'd like to meet' gambit.

There were more empty than full bottles between the food stains on the tablecloth. This was very good, and we had yet to order dessert. Perhaps Bruno and Carol would yet go out together for more wine, and take overly long to return. The 'trusted stranger' syndrome set in and my friends began to confess details to each other:

'I used to think English flowering plants were called "anglosperms",' Pete was telling Helen. 'The first couple of times I saw "angiosperm" I thought it was a typo.'

'I once fucked an English sailor – gee, what made me remember that …? Ha-ha. In the morning he spent half an hour ironing his uniform,' Helen contributed. 'What was his name? "Abel" or something …'

In the midst of my almost-solved dilemma about Carol and Bruno, the restaurant lights went down and the waiter carried a cake in, with candles and sparklers. A chef stood in the doorway behind him. Everybody sang a rousing, slurring version of 'Happy Birthday', and a few people at other group tables joined in for the three cheers. I made a very short speech: 'Twenty-four is going to be great!'

I was trying to appear to catch Louise's eye unintentionally. I cut the cake and made my too-obvious wish. I saw Louise was looking straight at me, so I sat down beside her again and reached for her hand. Our fingers wove together and our palms pressed tightly against each other as my friends passed the uneven wedges of cake around the table. I could heard Thomas muttering to Teresa, 'Orangeade? No one calls it that any more,' and they shared a confidential laugh.

PART III

PART III

Rock Platform

Distant thunder and Nat picked up her pace across the rock platform, around Dove's Head, though she was uncertain of the path's navigability on the western side or if a path to the top even existed. Maroon-tinged sky, clouds ringed her. Nat didn't like it because 'O' for ominous. No one about. She could've turned around. Didn't. She was the riskiest person on Earth. Big toe bled from stubbing on some bloody shell. Dammit. Or maybe a rock. She sniffed at the air like a frigging horse. Scent of rain? No idea, she thought. Who can even tell until it's falling on you?

The rock platform narrowed around the point, and Nat timed her traversal between sets of waves. Almost timed it. Quite good, but still got slightly splashed. Not really. She miscalculated completely, was decisively soaked. Kind of funny, so she kind of laughed. Anyway, she made it around. Platform got broad again, and she felt safer but wet stopped being funny. Plus, toe hurt.

On the western side of the point, the cliff-face appeared almost artificially smooth. Thirty metres ahead, or maybe twenty-five or forty, she saw another human, a plastic-pale man in a rock pool, not moving as the sky grumbled, still as bleached coral, continuing not to move as she felt tugged towards him. She was maybe fascinated by the intensity of his torpidity – not reciprocal, he didn't turn.

Hello? Nothing. Halloo. Nat stopped. Something weird about his head. Neck angle, maybe? Please, halloo. She took two small steps. Oh God or gods. Something was wrong, very wrong. Step. Such force in stillness, almost charismatic. Not charisma. Her face burned with the realisation, my God, this man's charisma had dissipated some time earlier. She knew, as though seeing death was the most natural thing in existence. Away spun her mind, it was weird, her death-recognition must've developed that week, shit, from all those TV crime shows she'd been watching, death after death. Step. Stop. I'm frozen here. She was now five steps from it. Him. So many bodies she had seen, but this one real. This one looked more plastic than any of them. Fuck. She wanted to touch it, touch him, and also didn't want to. Her hand extended and withdrew as though conducting thunder in the syncopated sky.

Shit, she thought. Storm's coming and deadman's here. She should take him, but how? How without touching him? Freaky, as though death could rub off, as though you could get some on you. She couldn't touch him, she couldn't, plus there was the whole don't-disturb-the-crime-scene thing. Step forward, step back, stop. No reception on her phone of course, this was a given, because now she was in this crime show, her show, maybe her show. Anyway, no phone reception meant no story and this, Nat was sure, was definitely story. She was still holding the useless phone. But oh yeah, not entirely useless. She crouched and took

192

a photo of him, of his pallor. Fascinated, she was, but that wasn't the right feeling. Terrible, to photograph his dead body. She held the phone towards him and tapped the button again. Sea was in the background. Hair whipped across her cheeks. She looked at the image on her phone. Evidence of something, she assumed. But there were no wounds visible in her picture or on the (his) body. She had started to look. Now she crouch-walked around the rock pool, around the body. Tap, tap, pic, pic.

The phone's memory ran out. What else? She opened the photo app and deleted, what, ten pics of Amy. Enough? This was weird, deleting photos from the real world. She felt annoyed with Amy, who'd taken her phone and snapped off about eighty-eight selfies when Nat had asked her not to. Don't be a spoilsport, said Amy, still posing. Nat's annoyance resonated at this strange moment.

There was a scratch on the man's left arm, ridged pink against paleness. Not a death-wound, Nat thought. She zoomed in on it anyway. What if he had been bitten by a stonefish? Did they live in rock pools? Did they bite? She tried to think. This wind was intense. Whitecaps from here to the horizon. She looked at the man's glass eyes. Clouds in them. *I have to tell someone.* No bars on her phone. She began to walk – what else could she do? She looked back as if it would start to make sense after all and he might get up and stop being plastic and glass and TV, but he didn't and he stayed where he was.

Here, perhaps, was the way up, yes, scramble through undergrowth and get to a ridge. She did it, ignoring her toe and the wind and a thousand scratching bushes. She was perspiring with effort. Over her shoulder she could see him. More thunder now and then. From this distance he wasn't a man. Up, up. From the top she couldn't see him and she found herself on the edge of a golf course, still in bushes. Someone called, Fore! Stop, she said, stop.

A ball bounced past and she could see a man and a woman approaching on a little cart. She stepped out. Deadman, she said. Dead. She must have looked wild. Stop, said the woman, who wasn't driving. The man stopped.

Now, what's happened? said the woman. You seem upset.

Deadman, said Nat. She held her phone towards them, the photos. Look, a deadman.

He might not be, said the woman, squinting.

Yes, he couldn't move. He is dead.

Is he near? Shall we phone the police? the woman asked.

Yes, phone the police, said Nat. She had thought she might do this on her own, see something no one else could see, solve the case.

Would you like some water? the man asked.

Okay.

Give her tea, said the woman.

Tea? asked the man.

Okay.

With sugar, said the woman.

Okay, said the man. He poured milky tea from a silver thermos into the red plastic cup that doubled as its lid, and stirred in several spoons of sugar. Nat sipped. It was sickly, foul, but not too hot so she took another gulp.

Did you do it? the man asked, keeping his eyes away from her, as though it had just occurred to him that second.

What? Me? Oh God no, no, he was already there. I came around the corner and he was there, she said.

As if this wasn't going to happen, she thought, now I'll be the suspect for hours. She stared down at the ground, at her feet.

The woman was on her phone, saying Dove Head golf course and distressed young woman, not sure, didn't see it myself but she has photos, she showed us, she says he's dead, couldn't tell, just photos, yes we'll wait with her. No, she doesn't have any weapon, she has nothing, no bag, nothing. Not sure of state of mind. Could be anything, I'm no psychologist, wouldn't guess. What? I'll ask.

Do you need a doctor, sweetie?

No, it's stopped bleeding. Just need to wash it.

What?

Nat showed her the injured toe. See.

Maybe a paramedic would be good, said the woman. She's kind of confused. Or confusing, anyway.

Nat took a last gulp of tea and showed her empty cup to the man. Good-girl moment.

More?

Okay, she said. Tea, she never drank tea. How funny. This one she drank fast. Three gulps, gone.

Steady on there, said the man. Why don't you sit down?

Okay, said Nat, almost toppling backwards in her cooperation. She sat. Some time passed. She could hear a siren and she saw police running across the golf course.

He's down there, she told them. He's in a rock pool.

Can you show us? said the first cop.

Nat tried to stand up but her legs had stopped working.

195

Here, lean on me, said Cop Number 2, hoisting her upright.

You take it easy, said the man.

Nat took one moment to realise he was speaking to the police, not to her.

Thanks for your trouble, said Cop 2, also not addressing Nat. We'll take good care of her.

So, said Cop 1, where we heading?

Down, said Nat.

Light rain was falling steadily now. Nat felt as though she could sense each tiny drop on her face, and all the drops cohering. So sensitive.

Is there a path? asked someone.

No, just go that way, Nat heard herself reply, or probably herself. She took a few steps towards the scrubland she'd climbed through maybe half an hour earlier.

Path? asked Cop 1.

Dunno, she said.

She sustained several more scratches. Toe wasn't bleeding.

From the ledge where they now stood, the man's body stood out like, *eeuw*, sashimi against the deep maroon of the rock platform. Terrible to think that. She tried to think something else. He might get up. Waves broke around it. Him.

I'm calling in a chopper, said Cop 2.

Yep.

Her hair was wet through, and the cop's, who held the police hat in her hand.

You hearing this? Over, said Cop 2.

Loud and clear. Over, said a voice, neither loud nor clear.

Nat laughed.

Shhh, said Cop 1.

We've got one suspected deceased, said Cop 2. Cause unknown. On platform below Dove Head, near the point. Request chopper. Urgent, incoming tide. Request Forensics.

Have a code 33, request chopper, request CSSB. Over.

Suspected 33.

Roger that.

Roger, said Nat.

Shhh, said Cop 1, again.

Okay, maintain your location. Sending it, rasped the voice. Over and out.

Out.

Okay, said Cop 1, once the helicopter arrives, we'll be taking you in to the station.

Me? Why?

Take your statement. All very standard.

Why?

No, no. We ask the questions. You answer.

Wait. I have to wait for the rescue. What if they need help? We have to go down.

No, said Cop 1, resting a hand on Nat's shoulder.

No, don't touch me, said Nat.

She twisted away and began to climb down.

Stop, said Cop 1. Stop immediately.

I have to, said Nat, not stopping.

I'll have to arrest you if you continue. I'm telling you to stop. You must comply with my reasonable directions in the interests of your own safety.

No.

Nat had put five or ten metres between herself and the police officer.

I'm warning you. Last warning, said the cop. This is a declared crime scene.

I don't think so, called Nat over her shoulder. I don't see why you should decide these things.

Ed, said Cop 1.

Don't worry about it, said Cop 2. Nat, please stop, please. But if you go, take care as you climb down. It's raining. It's slippery.

What the fuck, said Cop 1.

I know. Sorry, said Cop 2. You can see the state she's in.

All the more reason. Jesus. How are we going to get her back up?

It'll be okay. I've seen these before.

Me too, but I draw different conclusions.

Nat climbed down, turning away from the heaving ocean, backwards, so bushy here, so many ferns, and made her way towards the rock pool. She thought she could hear a helicopter though it wasn't yet in sight. She looked around, at the two blue figures zigzagging down the cliff, ignored them, began to wave her arms overhead like an air traffic controller.

The cops arrived.

That was silly, said Cop 1. You could have fallen. Now we're going to have to climb back up.

A huge wave crashed over the platform, soaking the three of them, dislodging the dead man, now in the middle of the pool.

I'm going to have to secure the body, said Cop 1. You can look after [gesture], seeing as you're the reason we're down here.

Cop 2 gave a glare. The helicopter came low and loud over the cliff. Megaphone asked, You clear to secure the deceased?

Secure, thought Nat.

Cop 1 raised a thumb. A wave sent foam high above them.

Come on, shouted Cop 2 to Nat – why was he shouting? Let's watch from a bit higher up.

I want to go in the helicopter, said Nat. I found him. I want to go with him.

No. It's full, shouted Cop 2. But we'll drive you in.

How do you know? She didn't trust anyone. Sort of. They'd retreated maybe five metres. A wave knocked Cop 1 over.

Whoa, said Nat. That was a big one.

Cop 1 tried to get up, but fell again, very hard. There was lightning, and Nat had the idea that the lightning had knocked the blue woman over.

Whoops, said Nat.

A rope dropped out of the helicopter.

Retrieving two, said someone, or maybe it was just her thought.

Wait here, shouted Cop 2, taking a few steps through the swirling air towards his unmoving colleague.

Stay back, came the megaphone. Retrieving two *only*.

Let's go, it's too dangerous here, Cop 2 shouted.

No, said Nat.

Don't make trouble, shouted Cop 2, trying to take her arm.

Nat was stronger than she looked. She twisted away and ran a few steps onto the rock platform.

Stay back, repeated the megaphone from the sky.

An orange shape now dangled from a rope. There was so much noise. Nat took a couple of steps towards the rock pool, which was still frothing from the last wave. Cop 1 hadn't moved since the fall.

Step back now. Danger, you are in danger, said the megaphone.

I'm going to help, said Nat into the sea spray.

A force hit her, and she fell.

What the fuck are you doing, the cop's voice shouted into her ear.

I'm helping, she said, perhaps too quietly to be heard.

A wave crashed over them, and she was scratched and bleeding everywhere, that's what it felt like, the blue man still gripping her.

Get off, she said. She lifted her head but Cop 2 wasn't letting go this time.

To her right, the orange shape had become a man, and he was harnessing the limp blue shape of Cop 1.

Come on, said Cop 2. Fuck.

He had her by the collar. She tried to hit his arm away, but no effect. The next wave's parabola was steeper, and they were soaked again, but at least not flattened.

Come on, said Cop 2 again. Nat had stopped resisting.

Blue and orange shapes ascended into noise above. The rock pool was empty. Over her shoulder, Nat glimpsed what might have been someone or something swimming or floating into the angry jade ocean.

His Boots Move Forward
as the Ground Stays Still

With each step along the white, crusted-clay bush track, dust exploded in a small way around his ankles. The boy, perhaps eight years old, could feel the movement of the dust particles. It was so frigging dry. He heard someone say that in a movie and thought it sounded cool. *It is so frigging dry.* Yeah. This is what the kid was thinking: *frigging dry* and *frigging hot* and *frigging trees.* Kids are funny, how they believe in transformation, how they have faith that they can transform themselves. They squeak out in their little voices the same muscular, perspiring phrases they've heard some rasping, deep-voiced actor boom out in a high dramatic moment, and in their heads it sounds exactly as effective and authentic. Out loud the boy said, 'Frig this heat.'

The sun, directly overhead, heated the track to a shimmer, as it sloped through the trees and sparse undergrowth. The boy swiped at a couple of flies with no real intent. He wasn't that murderous – no, really. He didn't care what the flies did, as long as they stopped bugging him. He was a pretty good kid, for a kid. They were eucalypts, those trees, and a half-decent botanist could have narrowed the boy's position down to a within a state or habitat or altitude by identifying which species had lasted beside that path. Nothing alpine, that was for sure. The kid, obviously, had no clue about eucalypt species. All kids are clueless about everything.

For example, the kid thought that 'frig' derived from 'refrigerator', so that 'frig the heat' meant something like 'refrigerate the heat'. That etymology explained exactly what he would have liked his imitation–actor words to do and made perfect sense to the kid with his cluelessness about what was sense and what was nonsense. It pleased him for a moment, that heat could be mechanically cooled at the utterance of three words. *Yeah*, he thought to himself, doing that self-barracking thing he had to do, spending so much time alone.

The boy switched from thinking about frigging or fridging the heat to thinking about his feet. He was watching the tips of the big boots kicking forward through the dust. Step, puff, step, puff. The boots. Hoo-boy, there was *no way on this planet* that he was going to turn around and go back where he'd come from in those boots. Ha-ha to the old man. Or just Ha! The boots kicked forward of their own will, without him causing their movement, so it seemed to him. These were one-way boots. He was thinking about how although his feet stayed clearly in view and the ground seemed to disappear behind him, he knew it was the ground which was keeping still while he was moving further and further from the old man's hut. His brain insisted upon the truth despite the false evidence of his eyes. *Yeah*. That was a revelation or an insight.

The heat was bothering him, and his lack of preparation wasn't helping. Not that he could have prepared himself much better. There was no time. And there was that other kid thing, that kids never prepare anything for anything. The old man had often claimed to be prepared for any eventuality. That was the thing about old men. They were very sure of themselves for no reason. Every step the boy took proved how wrong the old man was.

The boy remembered water because he was thirsty and there was no water to be seen. *Don't think of water*, he told himself, which was useless advice as he was already thinking of water and couldn't stop. He listened out for the sound of a creek, and for a moment mistook the hot wind rustling hot trees for water, but it wasn't, and on he went, stamping the dust into the air with each boot swing.

Swing-stomp. Swing-stomp.

He pictured himself from outside, as though he were in a cartoon on the television. There was a small boy trudging along a rocky path. His boots were way too big and he was wearing a camo hat. For a quarter of a second he could have been a hero army boy, taking after his dad or his uncle. But he wasn't. He was too dusty and there was no one to ruffle his hair at the end of the march. That television with its cartoons was the best piece of furniture in the hut.

He concentrated on the wide, sun-bleached path. He looked like he was striding out, at pace, but given the size of the boots relative to the size of the boy he couldn't have been. If he'd tried to walk quickly-hut-hut-at-the-double he'd have fallen out of the oversized boots, whoosh, somersault, limbs in all directions and boots flying either side of the burning path. Yow, yow, step, step, trying to grab the boots, sharp rocks and hot path, but he's got them back, even though they hadn't come off. And at that pace, his cap, also several sizes too large, would have unscrewed itself from his head and thwapped onto the ground, traced a two-thirds arc around its rim and sagged into the dust like a soccer ball which had given up on life. The boy would've had to turn around like some huge slow beast to go and retrieve it, the dust angling away from his skidding great boots.

He didn't speed up and he didn't trip. Step after loose-booted step, the boy stayed upright and held his momentum – he had two kinds of impetus, from his pace and from his determination never to see the old man again. He had his rhythm and he stuck to it. It worked. The shaky old camo cap never tipped off. His eyes remained shaded, unlike his forearms and his back. He was parched and kept wishing he'd thought to bring a water bottle. Maybe the path had once been a dried-out riverbed. He had no way of divining water. (Also: no bucket.)

It was as hot as it had ever been. The boy knew it, but it had been hot the previous day too. When he had set out that morning he knew it would be hot, but still he hadn't prepared. Although he was just a kid, he could regret things in his way.

The boy wore his shirt like a cape, with only the second-top button buttoned. It flapped out, even at his regular at-the-single pace, and the flapping of the cloth over his back felt almost like a breeze.

He picked up a small stone and thought to hurl it at a tree, which the stone's sharp edge might hit and chip the tree's bark. Instead, he threw it into the forest, where he could not see what it hit. He returned to watching the rhythm of his boots: he might have been walking for hours in those terrible old grey boots. Or brown. Or they might have been black once, if polished up in the quick-march-hut-two kind of way. He couldn't tell what colour they used to be or were meant to be.

It was so frigging hot. It had been hot all morning, all yesterday morning, all the mornings and afternoons which filled his kid-memory, hot for one day short of as long as the boy could remember, and even in the endless unforeseeable heat on top of the remembered and unremembered heat, he had no intention of stopping. He had walked further from the hut than he had ever ventured before and he was clear in his mind that he would never go back. If he was to be hot and dusty, let him be hot and dusty far from the hut. Once the old man realised the boots were gone, well, there would be another reason not to return, the thought of the old man's anger. Perhaps the old man already knew. Boots were rare. They were hard to find. Once upon a time the old man had promised the boy boots, but the promise had been for an almost unimaginable time far into the future, and the promise had not been mentioned since the dry times began soon after the beginning of the boy's memory.

As to what was out there, far ahead and with no prospect of return, the boy had decided not to believe the old man's stories. Beyond the edge of what they knew were toxic men who turned children into slaves. The stories told of vicious-fanged creatures of all sizes and of places where anything of beauty only served to hide ugliness. In other places, there was no true humanity. People who seemed sweet were always heartless and unreadable in the end. The boy had outgrown the moral of the old man's stories, which was always the same: *However bad it is here, out there is worse.*

Several hours passed. With each hour, the prospect of the old man tracking him down diminished. If only the boy could walk for seven or eight hours in that ridiculous footwear he would be free, at least free from the hut and the old man. How far would he travel? Ten kilometres? Twenty? That was a long way. What was the old man's range? Surely the old man had never been beyond four or five. In the good times a few kilometres was far enough. You could find what you needed. Why else condemn the world, unless you had everything already? Why would you condemn places you knew nothing about other than that they could have been the same as everywhere and the same as home?

In this heat, who had the strength to go further, who but the boy? As to whether he would find a way to survive, that would depend. He had only wanted to move from where he had been. To that extent, he had already succeeded. Now, though, the boy was very hungry and very, very thirsty. If only he had been older and had planned. If only he'd taken food and drink and something to shelter under. If only he knew where to go to seek help. If only he had been no longer a child.

He followed the track down a gentle slope. It swerved left around a corner ahead of him, and as the boy approached the bend he could sense coolness flowing towards him, sweeping between the trees to embrace him. A feeling from before, from some time before the time he could remember, came rushing up at him along with the drop in temperature. That sensation lifted his eyes from the path and the rhythmic kicking forward of the toes of his boots along it and he saw it all at once.

It took him five seconds to strip down to his shorts: cap off, boots off, shirt-cape off. He jumped in. Water. Fresh water. He sank into it and drank and played and swam and was overtaken.

Frogspeak

There is no point jumping in front of a roaring yellow bulldozer. It won't stop. It keeps vomiting diesel smoke and moving in whichever direction it was moving before your attempted intervention. It screams like a hundred thousand egrets crying 'frog, frog, frog' and then you don't exist anymore. You're dead like my mother. The volume drops, perceptibly. No space for amphibian sentiment, I can tell you.

If I eat every day, I will continue to live. That is my theory. See a bug, nab it, swallow it up. It feels so solid moving across the gullet, so substantial. I could eat all night except I fall asleep and I wake up having forgotten the last meal and my childhood.

I wish we weren't shifting to cement ponds. Why are we moving? I wish I could remember things: was the food always like this? Did insect larvae always have that slight metallic taste? Is it my imagination? I have no idea what's to happen next.

In the old days, so the choruses go, there was plenty of food. There were millions of mosquitoes which would sing a little 'eat me eat me' tune so we could find them hovering above the marsh, and they never diminished in number and they were always tasty and full of blood. Frogs grew to fifty times as big and when we hopped across the Earth, we left deep indents. One frog was larger than the others and when it rained this frog's footprint filled with water and became the bay.

That's the history in the frogcalls. My ten thousand cousins chant about the time before predators, the time when the world was only for us. They sing of the arrival of the birds, in a flock which darkened the sky and wiped out my forebears' cousins. These amphibians are gone and will not return. The wise frogs hid under rocks and took on the characteristics of aquatic plants and sang like the wind instead of like frogs and only sang at night and hid and hid and hid for epochs until the birds starved and only a few remained with probing beaks to torture my surviving ancestors.

New insects flew past, or tried to, but my ancestors leapt and caught them, tasted their slightly varied taste, their infinitesimal textural differences. There were new birds to dodge, birds with longer beaks or curved beaks or beaks which moved too swiftly to see. But always there were survivors, as proved by my presence. We are known as tenacious, and why shouldn't we be?

My parents lived on garbage juice, sipping at the metallic river, skipping from brick to sludge-coated brick or slipping into the thick green puddles, and always there was sufficient and they were neither happy nor unhappy, calling out to each other and all the others at night, the song being 'here, here, here, here'.

There is a little slipway from the brickpit through to other ponds. The further I swim the thinner the water, until

I have almost forgotten viscosity, can kick freely. The creek is new, the water always changing and no longer stinking of rotting chicken and rancid cauliflower but of sweet sand and river grasses. I am of course suspicious. Utopia is a place which is also no-place.

I suspect everything. I suspect the pure water and the glistening insects. I suspect the neat placement of convenient rocks on which to rest. I suspect the new songs, which despite retaining identical vigour to the old songs have absence at their heart. The frogs sing 'here, here, here' but I discern the lyric as 'here? here? here?'

I do not understand the new mountains which all but cover the stench of lettuce and beef kidneys. Not having seen the trees uproot before, I do not understand the migrating dance of the giant Moreton Bay fig trees. I cannot comprehend the diesel singing of the yellow metal aliens, the rise of perfectly smooth, perfectly hollow arenas in which the humans run in neat arcs. I suspect that this world is not the world into which I hatched and grew. I suspect that my cousins are not my cousins but transformed demi-frogs without history or stories. I suspect the perfect birds which never find my hiding place are false birds and the tasty flies are stuffed with alien pollen. I have no sense of place but only of emplacement. I suspect I too am dead.

The Monitors

'I give warning that I shall not here give the essence of every perception ... I shall confine myself ... to the character of fictitious, false, and doubtful perception, and the means of freeing ourselves therefrom.'
Benedict de Spinoza, *On the Improvement of the Understanding*

We stood around the microtome, which had broken down halfway through sectioning a batch of onion-skin-thin liver tissue for mounting. I believed the fault was in the belt mechanism, but Colin thought the blade had come loose. Eric informed us that the last person to know everything was the philosopher Leibniz, and he had died in 1716. The surface of the only cover-slipped slide seemed to be painted in brilliant, fluorodescent hues of green-yellow and red. The tissue resembled a compound of hornet, grasshopper and shrimp cells, magnified enormously. Not good. Dye extrusion fault?

'Put out a press release headed "New Species: Techo's Chance Discovery", and send it over to Bacteriology,' Colin suggested.

Too late. I'd discarded the slide and started systematically working back along the conveyor. One-two-three, perfectly trained. I did not respond to Colin but told Eric, 'You mean western knowledge.'

Eric retorted, 'Is there any other kind?'

Colin started listing, naming Caribbean and Pacific islands or Asian nations after each piece of information.

'Right-o. Enough,' snapped Eric.

'You would say that, anyway,' Colin told him, shirtily.

'Big deal,' said Eric, exaggerating his slight French-Belgian accent to quote the relevant European thinker: '"A body without soul is a body assisted by technical prostheses."'

'Yeah,' said Colin. 'Right.'

Eric's lips drew into a slow-mo sneer as he readied himself to continue, but an alarm signal from 2B terminated the conversation. Eric and I rushed out; Colin followed with the toolbox.

Later, at the pub, Colin commented, 'I bet that Leibniz guy didn't know many folk songs.'

I wasn't yet too drunk and was trying to balance loyalties. I said, 'He spoke ninety-four European languages.'

'Sure he did. You wouldn't know a dialect from a vernacular. Anyway, listen to this—' he pulled a dog-eared volume from his coat pocket, pretending he'd just thought of it: '"The water that beats down with the persistence of a metronome and makes dough of the houses is like the daily paper, it's a sodden idea that our minds can be purged of prejudices." Nino Majellaro. Italian.'

I could hardly drag my eyes from the pub screen, where impressionistic dogs charged around a pixelated track.

'*Sodden?*' I said.

*

Next night, observing the operation from Monitor Room One, the pub TV scene repeated.

'This signal must have gone through a blender,' Eric complained.

'Press RGB. That'll clarify it,' I suggested.

'Watch it on the small monitor, for Chrissake,' Colin mumbled, but tried to fix it anyway.

'Can we have some volume? The sound. No, a little more, not yet.'

'Yeah, that's it for sound.'

'It's not real clear, is it?' Colin backed away for a better view. 'Can hardly make out a goddamn thing, not that I can see past the end of my nose in the first place.'

The surgeon had turned entirely blue: clothes, skin, hair. In fact, everything was blue and no one else seemed to notice, or it didn't bother them if they had. I was imagining some old-time supervisor growling, 'My boy, this would irritate the crap out of you if you were competent.'

But there was no supervisor. We were responsible for ourselves. (First-year training manual, Introduction.) Soon, Colin found us some colour, but the red had come apart from the green.

'How many lines per inch are you supposed to get on this fucking thing?' Eric griped. 'Can't you adjust it, like move the screen forward or something? It's really hard to see. Flip to the other circuit, maybe.'

'What channel are you on, mate? You ought to relax.' This from the orderly, who shouldn't even have been there. 'Or are you right off the air?'

Colin came close to losing it. He was concentrating on

the wiring, as he always did when the signal fell apart. He was holding four or five different screws between his lips, and loops of wire were hooked around his neck. He glared at the orderly, who couldn't have had any idea of what was involved, but didn't speak to him. Finally the picture was good enough: the whirr of surgical hands across the patient's chest.

I was filling in time with self-accusations and self-confessions. Work was damaging. The constant pauses provided too much space for abstractions: 'I acknowledge a great fear of anything that will distract me from my studies or interfere with my habits. I am overcome by spasms of depth/shallowness, by the constant recession of the *mutaplying* image, by smoke and the stink of beer. I am lost in the invisibility of that big, falling-apart screen.'

The whole surgical-video thing washed over me in giant waves of fatigue. Our beery, bleary eyes unconsciously decoded the red/green and assembled an entire ... oh, who knows what we saw. The orderly tried to be funny, but he wasn't. It was pretty straightforward this operation, not much more than an exploratory. The orderly, in a nasal whine, took up the call: 'And there she is, her offsider is hosing the mud off, she's ready for it again and the barracker beside me really believes this is competitive sport, he really believes observing this is analogous to watching the operation of class society, he really hopes the snobby bitch pins her.'

'For Chrissake,' said Colin.

'On that size monitor,' said the orderly, 'you could miss the whole pointillism.'

★

Meanwhile, I had learned to see the actual flesh on the actual screen and could not stop interpreting those pictures. Would Sir Thomas More have picked up the idea as quickly as I had – I mean once he got over the shock of being transported through time and all that? Did an Ancient Egyptian see the paintings around Luxor as likenesses? Or some other form of representation? If a machine was programmed to print 'I am in state A' when in state A, how did this differ from (a posited) Jones saying, 'I am in pain' (or something as automatic) when in pain? I was too caught up in the patients' feelings, said the counsellor at debriefing. I was supposed to chant something like, 'I want none of this involvement.' I ought to have wanted to watch the procedure, for it to be over with, and to have returned to the cedar-veneer saloon bar for the salt on the peanuts, the satyriasic cartoon kick-boxers, and the young man in front of me in the betting queue, who rasped, 'My lover doesn't love me' to the betting shop attendant, watching the attendant's eyes as she handed over the last blue ticket of this day's losing streak, and her fingers briefly touched his palm.

Work, as with human relations, rarely turned out to be simple. I hardly ever left on time. The building, despite its apparent solidity, merely masked the circuitry: it was a proto-hospital of copper wiring and optical fibres. We moved from filament to filament, checking that an invisible non-substance functioned even while the false, voluminous hospital smothered patients and their visitors with the architecture of reassurance. Every procedure was driven by finely calculated allowances for mechanical failure and the infinite gradations of human error, so that whether the scalpel entered at one particular site, or at another site a micron further over, the patient would live. Signal fibres passed between the walls through narrow, temperature-stabilised tubes. Wires staple-gunned above the ceiling led to green, whirring fluorescent tubes. Finer filaments, stretched out below our feet as we half-ran between monitor rooms, sent tiny, green wave patterns across little green monitors. This sense of hospital absolutely cancelled out the masonry for me. It was a predatory logic which once acknowledged could not be set aside. My job became holding up the building, divining every hint of potential metal fatigue. Any screen flicker might have been significant. My shift would finish, but work went on and on.

Eric leaned forward, pressed the white button and said evenly to the pick-up, 'We've got no channel three. Repeat. We've got a problem with channel three.'

I got his voice distorting back at me through the headphones like a radio just off the station. White gowns converged on the torso, obscuring my view of the prone figure. Only its feet in their absurd green plastic slippers stuck out between two surgical gowns. Not that it mattered: I had other things to keep an eye on. They were swinging arms, pumping, counting out loud, flipping electrodes to On. At four-second intervals, someone shouted, 'Now!' The volume of that was way outside my headphones' capability. It was all attack.

I was trying to shake the noise out of my ears without removing the headphones when a row of minuscule, yellow glass hemispheres lit up in front of me.

'Yellow's on,' I proclaimed.

'Gotcha,' said Eric, who thought that a better thing to say than 'thanks'. But he didn't do anything until he saw it on his own screen. When it was okay, he pressed that green button again and said, 'That channel's firing. Repeat. Channel three's happening just fine.'

'Good,' said someone.

There were no other disturbances the rest of that shift. I believe the figure through the glass survived.

At the pub, Colin was explaining the ontological distinction between broadcast TV and cable. The pub screen was behind him. On it, spotty anglers reeled in spotty fish with grotesque jaws; interspersed were close-ups of lures and thirty-second lessons in attaching hooks to lines. I was filling the space between beer-swallows, saying 'Mm, mm' to Colin whenever he said, 'Y'know?' and going to the bar every other time we drained our glasses. I couldn't stand watching these people fishing, but I had no concentration left to listen to Colin. I begged the bartender to change channels and she said, 'Yeah, just a minute,' but did nothing because she had decided I would soon be too drunk to care. I was trying to argue with her. I was saying, 'I always care. Always.'

She smiled. 'I can tell, mate. I really can.'

I found myself going over and over all the material we were supposed to know. All this covert stuff about getting secrets that never should have been secret anyway across to the other side. The plot was usually generic: 'I met Roschinksy at the Hotel Nord at 7.00 p.m., and he handed me the sheaf with the antidote formula. Glancing at it, I immediately knew it was false. There was no nausea suppressant anywhere in the list of ingredients. Earlier, in Berlin, 1965, we found the Russians had blocked up the pinhole for our probe microphone.'

The old surgeons thought the comprehensive approach was wonderful, so different from what they went through, and especially the cameras and fucking condenser mikes all over theatre. They loved it: they thought it was real C21 spy tech. Every senior doctor in the place had anecdoted me about the mnemonics she or he devised to remember the musculature of the hand for final exams, and how much more profound the new system was, with its literary allusions and stories about leeches and barber-surgeons who made genuine advances despite adversity and near-total lack of hygiene.

Still, I was in no position to feel superior to them: I spent some nights in the monitor room, fell asleep with the headphones humming the dark surgeries into my head. I dreamed all these lines of coloured lights, patterns blinking, and in these dreams I understood what the patterns were saying. We were having a conversation, the patterns and I.

What did this mean I wanted? I couldn't figure it. Someone wrote – I must have read it as an epigraph somewhere – 'A compulsive thought is really a compulsive deed and the surrogate for an action.'

What was most bizarre was what the patients must have made of hospitalisation, surgery, ritual care: all the bindings-in, probes and pick-ups taped all over their bodies like sacramental medallions. They were lying there, absolutely loaded with IV morphine, sliding along hundreds of metres of Arctic White corridors. They must have been flipping out, running imaginary movies in their heads, as in: 'The wind picked up, flicking droplets of rain, sweat, oil through the wire mesh, I walked up Death Row for the last time, turned into the execution chamber, and was strapped into the Chair by two guards I had never seen before.'

Next second, the patients were out to it, but the brain activity continued. We were sitting there in the fucking monitor room, and the little screen kept flickering. We could see someone was in there, blood laced with all these demi-poisons, and they were still producing millions of brainwaves. We were supposed to keep an eye on it, and we did, but what can anyone really know? All these squiggly lines on the monitor had to correspond to something going on inside those brains: 'Thousands of years pass on Tharda. Forces of change conspire against the planet's rocky surface, cracking and grinding mountains to boulders, boulders to sand.'

If only those probes were a little more sensitive. This was how to see the world without leaving Australia ... at the early opener, guitars strumming away in the background, the station logos beckoningly personal. No wonder Leibniz was so confident. He must have had it right (quoting Ovid): *Omnia jam fient; fieri quae posse negabam.* Everything will now happen which I declared to be impossible.

Short Twos

Two Dismissals
Elizabeth Lee's former optometrist counselled her, 'Your expectations of sight are too high.'

Cut
Dr Cohen wasn't looking where he was going, stepped around the corner and almost ran into two young men, not looking where they were going either. *Esprit de temps.* The apologetic-looking one opened his mouth to say something and Dr Cohen prepared himself to wave off the apology – but instead the man said, 'Get fucked,' and the two were laughing as they carried on.

Dr Cohen called after them, 'That wasn't polite,' though he thought it was funny too, but they had already gone.

Repetition
'Don't make me tell you again,' said another father. This made no sense to the boy, who was not making anybody do anything.

Margins

At the furthest point of my house, the eastern balcony, where the goats dwell – we've got a herd of goats on the balcony, but it's not cruel, they like it, what with the view and the good company – I was sharing a newspaper article about a disturbance at the heliopause, which is the boundary of the solar system. 'Postcards from the edge', it was headlined, echoing the title of some old book in the way that newspapers do, when they wish to induce a sense of familiarity.

The goats generally respect me. So far as staying up to date with happenings throughout the universe, not to mention the local paper, I am at the cutting edge.

But why was this news? asked one of the goats (the intelligent, dappled one who is secretly my favourite). Surely there are immeasurably frequent off-Earth disturbances at all times.

Apparently, it was news because the disturbance had been observed by a couple of Earth-sent spaceships. Everything has to be about us. And until this disturbance occurred, no one knew where the boundary was. As I admitted to the goats, I didn't even know there *was* a boundary, and am disappointed that there is, that we float around in a different kind of space to 'out there', that we are able to call ourselves central again. Accompanying the article, there was even a dinky little diagram of the solar system, with a couple of arrows to represent the paths of the spacecraft that had observed the newly observable.

I folded the newspaper and placed it near a few strands of straw. I was telling this goat that, some time ago, I had lost track of what the people I know were doing. There were simply too many people accumulated over too many years to remember. I began to forget names, though the faces remained familiar. Sad, sad, the puzzled faces which asked me why I was so distant. The goat nodded sagely. It's not as if we can send little inner-spacecraft out there into the world to monitor our relationships, to report back about disturbances at the edge. We're supposed to intuit these sorts of things. At least the goat understood why *I've* been so on edge, despite remaining on Earth.

Ah, the goat tried to reassure me, but it's the margins which define the centre, or the centre defines itself in relation to the margins, so really the margins are just as central as the centre and we're all the same and the world's a paradise just in need of a little fine-tuning.

Sure, I responded (also trying to reassure myself), and the other thing one might say is that it's all a matter of scale: the universe, this solar system, an atom of hydrogen. A flea, according to John Donne, contained all anyone needed to know about love. Observe the behaviour of a hive of bees over several lifetimes and you will understand human or goat society. In 'Chaconne for a Solipsist', the poet Michael

Dransfield wrote that for some there are no margins, there is only the self, that nothing else exists outside the room (or, implicitly, the balcony) in which a human (or a goat) occupies the moment and also that everything is incredibly trippy – but not in terms of an actual journey where we might be confronted with our essential smallness.

My goat, who's a sort of expression theory poetry critic, thought that I was trying to tell it something gently, what with the poem containing a reference to a glittering exit held in its speaker's hand. I assured the goat that no such fate was in store for either of us, and, anyway, the reference wasn't to a knife. We will all remain central, our solar system making the front pages of all known newspapers. The goat was very satisfied with this. So please: don't ever let anything change.

A Thousand Plateaus

Where I come from, there's reason to fear the vegetation. Where I come from, the grains of pollen are the size of peas. I'm talking leaves the size of the Pacific plate. I'm talking flowers the size of continents. I'm talking big enough to do whatever they want to do. Where I come from, the plants are a law unto themselves.

Walter Badheim, the cherry tree, doesn't pay me any attention today. It is irritated that I have tethered it to the water tank rather than letting it wander off among the goats. I absolutely drown its roots in fertiliser but nothing will please it. My heart is breaking. It drinks nothing.

Drink, please drink, I plead. But as I said, Walter is ignoring me. Other plants lean towards me as I pass, as though full of Walter's malign intent. *I can explain*, I tell them. That hissing sound, perhaps I am imagining it.

This town is a satellite. When a town is a satellite, it is not a satellite like the moon. It has no phases. It never moves a muscle. It sits quietly in the middle distance, having its air interfered with by the bigger city in the foreground. Sometimes I dream of shifting into the foreground city, as if by moving I would become closer to myself. But I have read there are too few plants in that place, and to move from a town to that city would not be so simple – what with centrifugal force and the great dome of foliage which is part of the sky.

So here I am cooped up in a satellite town with weak air and a whole battalion of plants threatening to overthrow me. Nevertheless, the town is resilient as hell and like hell it never stops burning. Things are looking, as we say here in crisis times, badly distinctive.

Out the window you can see it is getting dark. Dark as anything. This is not due to the onset of night, nor to Walter having broken free from its bonds – the cherry tree remains where tethered. Darkness is occasioned by seed clouds flying towards the sun. Darkness is a sign of our decaying morals and standards and failing discipline and our growing willingness to allow the wandering of unethical and poorly behaved plants among the goats. (Increasingly, all their floral thoughts are pernicious.) Darkness is also due to the approach of the evening meal and of its bringer. The azaleas, the only angiosperms not holding out for better conditions, join us at table and receive blood and bone. My landlord carves his beef with relish.

'Any work today?' he enquires with a sneer. I thank Feronia, Roman goddess of spring flowers and vegetation, that I have only one landlord to hinder my every step.

(Silently:) *May his wishes turn to spinifex.*

We eat well. The scab azaleas burp appreciation. My landlord leaves without so much as a swinging left. A better breeze is blowing.

I am the only living thing remaining in the kitchen.

I withdraw a family-size apple pie from the freezer and microwave it until it's too hot to eat. I watch it cool – eventually steam settles around its plate like an evening mist – and spoon it bit by bit into my mouth. I finish the whole pie. This will be the lot of any plant which does not bow to my rule. I walk across the garden and trip over the Moreton Bay fig.

(Silent, pursed lips:) *You're barking up the wrong shins.*

I kneel before Walter. *Please.* I untie it. I offer one of the goats before it, but Walter does not respond, so the goat is spared for now. *Please.*

At midnight I go to the top of the hill and look out over the geology humans have wrought. I can see the city in the distance. It has been neatly pruned to provide a hedge for the ocean. On this side is the land. At night the trees are all but silent in their conspiracy. I can understand only an occasional word. The word is 'rise'. Tomorrow I must no longer compromise.

Art Life

Hey, this is cool. The woman in the window seat whose face is almost totally hidden by her long hair except that her nose and mouth protrude, exact profile – you know, 180 degrees – plus there's the backlit window silhouette thing going on, *plus* she's really still, *really* concentrating on listening, she's wearing earphone things, and after a while the chorus must come on, the rest of her totally unmoving, she's mouthing silently, and it becomes clear what she's listening to, when the chorus is happening, her entire person totally still except for her lips moving, yeah, making the shapes of the chorus of 'Beat It'. It's very funny. Like, she could be talking to me.

Angel

The teenager (angelic like all teens) says, 'You used to sound like yourself but now you sound like your whole family talking at once.'

The parent, likely thrice the years of protag number one, has no clue what the referent is, so says, '*A propos* of something mysterious.'

'Yes, Latin for no real response,' says the teenager. 'Let's get a move on.'

The parent is ascending the incline as fast as parently possible and the teenager knows it and/or is universally sceptical of all parental claims, including those as to maximum velocities.

'You can go ahead if you like,' says the parent.

'No, because you'll give me shit about it later,' says the teenager.

'No I won't.'

'Yes. You always do.'

Always, thinks the parent, means once and in very narrow circumstances, but no communicational purpose in trying to say anything about anything when they're in the moods they're in, the parent thinks – and by *they* the parent means the teenager.

Although the parent experiences the hill as steep, the perceived rate of acclivity varies from day to day for the teenager. On this particular afternoon marked by middle-aged gravity, the incline measures hardly a nudge above flat to the teen, who has compromised impatience with sighing virtue by walking a few steps ahead. What's with that? the parent wonders, or if *wonders* is too soft a word, *judges*.

The parent has sought advice about the varied slopes of their relationship and is, perhaps, a little deluded about the subject requiring such healing. The psychologist knows exactly, and has advised the parent to apologise to the teenager wherever possible. Apparently this costs nothing and may help. If so, the parent thinks, why does it feel so fucking difficult? The parent will raise this again in the square, tear-stained room, intermittently looking across at the practitioner of the art of controlled eye contact (expensively taciturn). That's in the foreseeable future. Now the parent calls out, 'Sorry, I'm so slow.'

The parent calls out, 'Are you hungry?'

'I don't know. Maybe. Getting hungry.'

Sometimes the parent feels hollowed out, as though only an exuvia remains, clinging to a vertical surface as the wind picks up. Is this visible to others? The teenager is more like overflowing, too much inside and too much outside, and no borders between the two so that everything out gets in and it's actually wrong to hold anything for long because there's too much.

They reach the crest, almost together.

Attributed to Jeremiah

If I told you half the things I know, you'd bawl your eyes out and if I told you the other half, you'd laugh your fucking head off. English is a dismemberingly cruel idiom, and it fits this world too well.

From fence to fence the suburb is uneven. A wall of brick and one of stone, a row of three with almost matching renders, the high sheen on the central span produced, perhaps, by a single over-zealous polisher; here is a gap and there impermeable, sealed off by a button and a lens. Nature derides these efforts. Ivy trains itself away from the windows, drags down garage doors to reveal half-restored sports cars or heaped tea chests garlanded with dust. Some unnameable subgeologic force heaves at the footpath till it breaks up into a confusion of creeping asphalt capillaries. And so on. (Look at it yourself.)

From behind the fences you hear love and violence, constrained or released, verbalised or silent, roaring or drip-fed, unceasing or stuttering, dreamed of or realised, proclaimed or secret.

Messengers (self-proclaimed) are all demeanour, no content, again and again. Look at me: I'm beyond categories.

The lonely walk among many and they walk alone. You are exiled from those, and those places, with whom, and where, you deserve to dwell and love. Your lovers or companions or children fail to visit because they will not or cannot or are no longer. No one goes where they ought to go and the innumerable trespass where they ought not. Those you admire go unrewarded and impostors recline like fallen trees at the table's head.

This *and* that for the righteous and the wicked. Thus sayeth those who sayeth these sorts of things.

(Focus.) The honourable appear drunkenly like buffoons; the gutters overflow in our sacred places; these places become like drains. Those you detest have laid their hands on your treasures, devaluing them forever. Their touching breaks all the laws of heaven and the laws you wished to make and live by on earth. There is no longer anything retaining value, not from horizon to horizon, not the nation, not the city, nor these people with their accumulations.

Your city shrieks like a princess, like a widow, like a wound.

The neighbours' voices produce the occasional word, hers hectoring, constant and angry; his is almost inaudible, but goading nonetheless. Then there's the usual afternoon cicada silence; you can't tell if they're in love again or if they've gone out. Later, they're at it again. Across the road, fourteen pairs of white underpants are neatly spaced along the clothesline, symmetrical as a joke. Two weeks bleached out in half an hour. And there is no third way, no middle path, no prospect of compromise between the two aesthetics of behaviour, incessancy and sparsity.

No one's laughing now, but it's a funny world when bananas have to be marked 'organic'. It's like the menace in the smile of a stranger, and as impure as taxonomies of anger. The streets cannot be seen through this furious mist, though they can be felt shaking with love and with violence and with mongrel blends of the two. We are all mourning and we have all earned the right. Passers-by bestow upon us their diminishing half-smiles or avert eyes for the embarrassment. They are like nothing, like tourists, and they witness nothing real. Without any memories they cannot distinguish this blank poverty from our former brilliance. The suburb is dressed in rags of mourning and the signs of mourning are as pervasive as its sighs.

From time to time the landlady comes knocking. She thinks to safeguard the house she believes she owns. It is destroyed from the inside out; the destruction is not yet visible and will be revealed.

All our ambitions, all our dreams, all our images of all our futures – these we have abandoned for a full gut and yet we remain hungry. Babies call for mash and for wine, scarcely knowing what food and drink might be.

I've seen plenty. We age like concrete, being thumped this way and that (this *and* that). Here are X-rays of my ribs following the car accident. Elsewhere are X-rays of my teeth, and of my right ankle, which I once broke in a fall. The X-rays. A few more injury records and I'll own the elements for a composite of my entire body.

I'm shot, shot to pieces. I'm crawling through fire-ruined flatlands where once stood something. I am beaten and poisoned and dust-covered and tricked. I am pathetic. You don't need divine vision to see that.

The passers-by allow a laugh now and then, sudden and brief enough to startle birds, but it's only punctuation for this English in which tears are like magnifiers and the world is too large to describe, or beautiful as a road gilded by the setting sun. Soft and mammalian as a road, too, and a strange vengeful beast with a brain like a hornet on a windless day.

Those pursuing us are too fast, and they have too many disguises and hiding places.

Where is the substance of which we are made? From this age, and with my experience, all of it, the advice to my twenty-year-old self would still not be clear cut. There are times for which I would say, 'Be more cautious,' and, for others, 'Be more impetuous.' I am working my way back through my life, imagining it without the errors.

Sometimes I believe it would have been better to err quickly and get the consequences over with. Sometimes I wish that once I had commenced my erroneous route, I had followed it to its end, aware, slow as an auditor, as slowly as an old man on a correct journey, as one of those incredible men who lived a century as though just beginning, and learned something every day.

Praying has never really suited me, though there is comfort in chanting and repetition. There is comfort in the community of chanters and repeaters.

And these are the chants: anything our forebears squandered we have outdone. We have wasted our ancestry. We have worked under the wrong premises and for the wrong rewards. We have been enthralled by the logic of bankers and surfers and by the logic of those who see commonalities among children and who see only crowds. We have eaten and eaten and eaten, eaten like secret termites undermining, and eaten like a scouting locust, the sight of which tells the future. We are burning and humiliated. We are silent and we cannot stop weeping. The land is taken by feral beasts.

And we hang on to our hopes like walls grasping at dust motes.

Acknowledgements

The following pieces have been previously published, broadcast or exhibited:

'War Against the Ungulates' first published in *Heat* magazine (new series, No. 17). Also published in *The Best Australian Stories 2008* (ed. Delia Falconer, Black Inc., 2008).

'The Chinese Meal Uneaten', *Asia Literary Review*, Autumn 2011.

'In the Time It Takes to Finish a Sandwich, We Could Build Worlds', *Southerly: Mixed Messages*, Vol. 77, No. 3, 2018.

'Waltzing Matilda' in *Hardly Beach Weather* (HarperCollins, 2002).

'Theatre of Soak', *RealTime* magazine.

'Foreign Logics' was commissioned by DA2 Digital Arts Development Agency as a collaborative installation with artist David Bickerstaff and exhibited at Lethaby Gallery (London), Institute of Contemporary Art (London) and several other galleries. Sections of 'Foreign Logics' appeared in an essay, 'Taipei, Expectant', in *Harvard Review*, Spring 2002.

'Orangeade', *The Best Australian Stories 2002* (ed. Peter Craven, Black Inc., 2002).

'The Monitors', published as 'Monitors', *Pub Fiction* (ed. Leonie Stevens, Allen & Unwin, 1997).

'Frogspeak', broadcast as 'Frogspeak: transplanted habitats at Homebush Bay' on ABC Radio National's *Radio Eye* arts and culture program.

The title 'Fire in My Brain, That You'd Like to Put Out' is taken from the song 'Buddy' by Peter Gutteridge, *Snapper* EP, first published by Flying Nun in 1988. I am grateful to the executor of Peter Gutteridge's estate for permission to quote this.

Thanks to Kathryn Heyman, Jane Malone and Beth Yahp for feedback in the assembling of *When I Saw the Animal*. For writing space and time, thanks to Varuna, the Writers House, and to Simon and Rebecca Ehrlich. Thanks to the Three Weedy Writers for writerly camaraderie, and to my students at The Writing Workshop for being excellent audiences for early oral drafts of some of these pieces. Thanks to my publisher Madonna Duffy, production editor Felicity Dunning and all the team at UQP. Thanks to Josh Durham for the terrific cover. Thanks to creative editor Felicity Plunkett for helping me select, edit and order the pieces in this collection.

Thanks to all my family and especially to my daughter Pola for being generally fab.

Also in UQP's short fiction series

PORTABLE CURIOSITIES
Julie Koh

Winner, *Sydney Morning Herald* Best Young Australian Novelist 2017

Brilliantly clever and brimming with heart, these twelve stories combine absurd humour with searing critiques on contemporary society – the rampant consumerism, the casual misogyny, the insidious fear of those who are different. *Portable Curiosities* is an unforgettable collection by a significant new talent.

'Cutting-edge writing in many ways.' Maxine Beneba Clarke, *Guardian Australia*, Best Books of 2016

'Koh is a gifted satirist who makes wonderful use of language ... in this clever and highly original collection.' *Age/Sydney Morning Herald*

ISBN 978 0 7022 5404 8